"Leo, fo[illegible]ber, I've had que[illegible]s death. Questi[illegible]en to my sisters. [illegible]er dated after she died? I have to find out why."

D0348533

"I can call my dad. He might remember something," Leo offered.

Bianca's eyes lit up. "That's a good idea. Maybe he can at least clarify things for us." She looked out toward the sea. "I'm thinking about hiring a private investigator, just to find out what I can."

"Regarding your mother?"

"Regarding my mother's death. Think about it—none of us has ever questioned our father's version of things. Maybe it's time one of us did."

* * *

THE SECRETS OF STONELEY:
Six sisters face murder, mayhem and mystery
while unraveling the past.

FATAL IMAGE—Lenora Worth (LIS#38) January 2007

LITTLE GIRL LOST—Shirlee McCoy (LIS#40) February 2007

BELOVED ENEMY—Terri Reed (LIS#44) March 2007

THE SOUND OF SECRETS—Irene Brand (LIS#48) April 2007

DEADLY PAYOFF—Valerie Hansen (LIS#52) May 2007

WHERE TRUTH LIES—Lynn Bulock (LIS#56) June 2007

Books by Lenora Worth

Love Inspired Suspense

Fatal Image #38

Love Inspired

The Wedding Quilt #12
Logan's Child #26
I'll Be Home for Christmas #44
Wedding at Wildwood #53
His Brother's Wife #82
Ben's Bundle of Joy #99
The Reluctant Hero #108
One Golden Christmas #122
†*When Love Came to Town* #142
†*Something Beautiful* #169
†*Lacey's Retreat* #184
‡*The Carpenter's Wife* #211
‡*Heart of Stone* #227
‡*A Tender Touch* #269
**A Certain Hope* #311
**A Perfect Love* #330
Christmas Homecoming #376

Steeple Hill

After the Storm
Echoes of Danger

†In the Garden
‡Sunset Island
*Texas Hearts

LENORA WORTH

grew up in a small Georgia town and decided in the fourth grade that she wanted to be a writer. But first she married her high school sweetheart, then moved to Atlanta, Georgia. Taking care of their baby daughter at home while her husband worked at night, Lenora discovered the world of romance novels and knew that was what she wanted to write. And so she began.

A few years later, the family settled in Shreveport, Louisiana, where Lenora continued to write while working as a marketing assistant. After the birth of her second child, a boy, she decided to pursue her dream full-time. In 1993, Lenora's hard work and determination finally paid off with that first sale. "I never gave up, and I believe my faith in God helped get me through the rough times when I doubted myself," Lenora says. "Each time I start a new book, I say a prayer, asking God to give me the strength and direction to put the words to paper. That's why I'm so thrilled to be a part of Steeple Hill's Love Inspired line, where I can combine my faith in God with my love of romance. It's the best combination."

LENORA WORTH

Fatal Image

Published by Steeple Hill Books™

If you purchased this book without a cover you should be aware that this book is stolen property. It was reported as "unsold and destroyed" to the publisher, and neither the author nor the publisher has received any payment for this "stripped book."

Special thanks and acknowledgment are given
to Lenora Worth for her contribution to
THE SECRETS OF STONELEY miniseries.

To Tina Hughes—an avid reader and a good friend

STEEPLE HILL BOOKS

ISBN-13: 978-0-373-87414-9
ISBN-10: 0-373-87414-6

FATAL IMAGE

Copyright © 2007 by Harlequin Books S.A.

All rights reserved. Except for use in any review, the reproduction or utilization of this work in whole or in part in any form by any electronic, mechanical or other means, now known or hereafter invented, including xerography, photocopying and recording, or in any information storage or retrieval system, is forbidden without the written permission of the editorial office, Steeple Hill Books, 233 Broadway, New York, NY 10279 U.S.A.

All characters in this book have no existence outside the imagination of the author and have no relation whatsoever to anyone bearing the same name or names. They are not even distantly inspired by any individual known or unknown to the author, and all incidents are pure invention.

This edition published by arrangement with Steeple Hill Books.

® and TM are trademarks of Steeple Hill Books, used under license. Trademarks indicated with ® are registered in the United States Patent and Trademark Office, the Canadian Trade Marks Office and in other countries.

www.SteepleHill.com

Printed in U.S.A.

A word was secretly brought to me,
my ears caught a whisper of it.
Amid disquieting dreams in the night,
when deep sleep falls on men,
fear and trembling seized me
and made all my bones shake.

—*Job* 4:12–14

Love alters not with his brief hours and weeks,
But bears it out even to the edge of doom.
If this be error and upon me proved,
I never writ, nor no man ever loved.

—*William Shakespeare*
"Sonnet 116," lines 11–14

ONE

Coming back to this house always made her think of her late mother.

Bianca Blanchard stood in the massive hallway of Blanchard Manor, a chill moving through her body as she handed her black velvet evening cloak to a nearby servant who'd been hired as extra help for this special evening.

Adjusting the tight-fitting bolero jacket of her navy-blue evening gown, Bianca searched the elite crowd for signs of her older sister, Miranda. She'd feel much better if she could talk to her. Bianca hadn't really wanted to come home to the quaint town of Stoneley, Maine, for their Aunt Winnie's sixtieth birthday party, but it would have been rude and downright unforgivable for her to stay away. She loved Aunt Winnie, as did all of the Blanchard sisters, but Bianca didn't enjoy parties. Especially in this house. She never had, and she probably never would. Entering a crowded room had always made her feel claustrophobic, as if she might die of suffocation. Entering the Blanchard house only added to that feeling.

In spite of the majesty and castlelike façade of the huge stone mansion sitting on the cliffs overlooking the Atlantic Ocean, the painful memories lurking about in the dark corridors, coupled with the sadness and sickness permeating the many rooms of the house, made it impossible for Bianca to put on a happy face and work the crowd.

To calm herself, she glanced around at the familiar things she remembered from her childhood. The sweeping walnut staircase opened wide with heavy, ornate balustrades, making Bianca want to run up those stairs and straight to the room she'd once shared with Miranda. That sunny room with the double bay windows on the second floor would be quiet and cozy, not nearly as dark and foreboding as the capacious downstairs parlor to her right and the long dining room to her left. Even crowded with the A-list guests of Stoneley society, the house still echoed with a melancholy that caused shadows to leap out at Bianca.

Shadows filled with memories of her mother.

But no one here was allowed to talk about that.

Bianca steeled herself, pretending she was in the courtroom preparing for opening statements on an important case. She had no problem standing up to ferocious judges or devious white-collar criminals, but she sure had a problem trying to fit in with this high-society crowd.

Smoothing her dark brown upswept hair, she looked across the hallway, past the round mahogany table decorated with a crystal vase full of white roses and baby's breath, her gaze moving over the many faces to finally settle on one.

Leo Santiago.

Bianca smiled, her gaze holding Leo's for a minute. He nodded his head, his blue eyes flashing with the intensity she remembered so well. A smile worked at his full lips as he watched her.

"Steady," Bianca whispered to herself, remembering how from the first time she'd met him, she'd always felt an intense awareness of Leonardo Santiago. Even though their paths rarely crossed, Bianca enjoyed the challenging banter that seemed to flow between them almost like a casual flirtation—if she only knew how to really flirt. But flirting with Leo wasn't so very hard, since he was a striking man. He always dressed impeccably, born executive that he was. And with thick sandy-brown hair and electric blue eyes, he could easily pass for a leading man in a romantic movie.

Maybe Leo could help her out tonight. She'd learned in high school speech class that a speaker should find one kind soul in the audience and make eye contact often with that person. That method had worked for Bianca with stoic jurors. Maybe it would also help her through an awkward social event. Especially since Leo didn't seem to have a problem making eye contact.

Dropping her gaze, Bianca could feel a slight blush moving up her neck. It made sense that her father's right-hand man at Blanchard Fabrics would be invited to her aunt's birthday party. Ronald Blanchard expected complete loyalty from his employees, and that certainly included ordering them to show up and make nice with some of the richest citizens of Stoneley.

She knew Leo's history with the town's famous textile and fabric mill. He'd worked his way up, laboring throughout high school and college, from factory worker to second in command. He was now a valuable assistant to her father. Leo's youth and business smarts had brought the company into the twenty-first century with innovative ideas in both synthetic fabrics and environmentally conscious technology, without compromising the integrity or reputation of Blanchard Fabrics.

Well, more power to him, Bianca thought as she finally spotted her sisters Miranda and Juliet coming toward her. Putting thoughts of Leo out of her mind, Bianca hugged Miranda close. "Hello."

"How are you?" Miranda, clad in a long-sleeved burgundy velvet dress, hugged Bianca close.

"More important, how are *you?*" Bianca asked back, concern for her older sister foremost in her mind.

Miranda suffered from anxiety attacks each time she left the mansion. She was a gentle, caring person, with a love of poetry, spending most of her time creating beautiful handmade chapbooks. Bianca wished Miranda could find a way to overcome her agoraphobia, so she could get out of this depressing house more often.

"I'm doing okay," Miranda replied. "No panic attacks so far tonight. And no disasters, party-wise, either."

"I'm here to give her moral support," Juliet told Bianca as she held Bianca's hand in hers and kissed Bianca on the cheek. "We all know Father isn't very good at that sort of thing."

Bianca didn't want to get caught up in their father's lack of affection for his six daughters. Not tonight, anyway. This was Aunt Winnie's special night.

"Well, I'm here to give my support," she said, "and I'm so glad to see both of you," Giving Juliet the once-over, she grinned. "I see you're being your usual rebellious self. A bit dressed down tonight, aren't you?"

Juliet made a face. "Hey, I'm glittery."

"You sure are, because you are such a jewel."

The sisters both groaned while Bianca admired Juliet's outfit. Her tunic was a sequined and sparkling white-gold, making her long, platinum hair shimmer even more, but her jeans were vintage and defiant. Juliet had her own version of formal attire, probably because one day she hoped to have her own brand of fashion designs. Bianca's youngest sister was attending fashion design school in Vermont, but planned to come home after graduation to work for Blanchard Fabrics.

"Come on in to the party," Miranda said, tugging at Bianca's hand. "Aunt Winnie has been asking about you."

They strolled toward the parlor where Winnie Blanchard sat by the roaring fire. The dark-paneled room looked festive and warm in spite of the cold, snowy January night. The family portrait hanging over the cavernous stone fireplace showed a smiling Howard Blanchard with his two grown children, Ronald and Winnie, the six young Blanchard girls, dressed in velvet and bows, sitting at their feet. To the casual observer, that portrait represented a large, loving family.

To Bianca, the absence of her mother from the picture represented a vast emptiness that flowed in its own unexplainable way through each of the Blanchard sisters.

As she stared up at the portrait, Bianca could clearly see what wasn't so obvious to the outside world. Howard Blanchard held power over his children, even now when he was frail and ailing. The fact that both Ronald and Winnie—one a widower and the other a self-proclaimed spinster—were still living under their father's roof, indicated that something wasn't quite right in Blanchard Manor.

Bianca's inquisitive mind had always wanted to find out what that something was, but she was so afraid of the answers she preferred instead to bury herself in work and stay away as much as possible.

Outside, the wind howled as a snowstorm moved over the area. Bianca could hear the rapping of a tree branch against the tall windows of the parlor. "Where is everyone else?" she asked Miranda, to stifle the chill going down her spine.

"Delia is with Aunt Winnie, trying to convince her to come to Hawaii for a summer vacation, last I heard," Miranda said, smiling over toward their younger sister and their aunt, both of whom now were so involved in a discussion with the brand-new, much talked-about Reverend Gregory Brown of Unity Christian Church, that they hadn't noticed Bianca's arrival. "And probably arguing religious philosophy with the new pastor, too."

Bianca watched as an animated Delia brushed a hand through her short, dark gamine bangs. "She looks happy," she said, glad to see the glow on her surfer sister's face.

Juliet held her arm tightly. "Portia and Rissa are in the kitchen, supervising the caterers, while Sonya tries to supervise both of them."

"Sonya Garcia must be as old as this house," Bianca said, smiling at the thought of the hot-tempered, scowling housekeeper still reigning over the entire staff. "She's been around forever, hasn't she?"

"Seems like," Juliet said, grinning. "Both she and the nurse, Peg, pretty much rule the roost around here. But the twins have such a New York attitude, Portia and Rissa love to go at it with both of them, just for fun."

Miranda gave them a mock-stern look, her schoolmarm persona coming through. "Be nice, girls. Sonya is very loyal to Grandfather, even if she does act as if she hates all of us. And Peg, well, she is so devoted to him, the rest of us have a hard time even getting into his room to visit him."

"Women are always loyal to the Blanchard men," Bianca pointed out, the bitterness in her words giving her an edgy tone as she thought about her once-robust grandfather now bedridden with Alzheimer's. Changing the bitterness into a prayer of hope, she asked, "How is Grandfather doing?"

"Not so well," Miranda said. "He rarely knows any of us anymore. Sometimes he says the oddest things. It's all part of the disease, but it's hard to watch." She gave Bianca a sympathetic look. "So don't expect much if you can get past Peg to visit him."

"I've never been one to expect too much from our father *or* our grandfather," Bianca said, then instantly wished she'd stayed quiet.

Howard Blanchard was old and ill. She

supposed she should show him some respect. But anger and regret colored any heartfelt feelings she might have conjured up for the grandfather who'd taken them all in here at Blanchard Manor after her mother's tragic death nearly twenty-three years ago. Their grandfather's generosity had come with certain stipulations and expectations. Bianca still had trouble trying to figure out what exactly the six Blanchard sisters had done to make their father and grandfather become so cold and cruel.

"I'm sorry," she told her sisters. "I'm just not in a festive, generous mood tonight. My bitter words aren't aimed at you two."

As if sensing her dark thoughts, Miranda quoted Shakespeare, something her poet's soul loved to do on a regular basis. "'By that sin fell the angels.'"

Bianca cringed. "I think that line from *Henry VIII* is more about ambition than bitterness, Miranda."

"I never could get one past you," Miranda said with a sweet smile. "I tend to forget that you love Shakespeare as much as I do."

Bianca laughed, hoping to lighten things. "Speaking of ambition, where is the lovely Alannah tonight?"

"Probably in the library with Daddy," Miranda replied, making her own scornful face. "I think he's giving her a special present tonight."

"It's not our father's girlfriend's birthday," Juliet

hissed. "So why does she always wind up with more presents than any of us?"

"She's the flavor of the month," Bianca said, keeping her tone very low. "Maybe she won't be around much longer."

"Let's drop it," Juliet retorted. "Why don't we go and speak to Aunt Winnie?"

"Good idea," Miranda said, pushing them forward. "I'm going to check on the music. I specifically asked that ensemble to play some of Aunt Winnie's favorites from the fifties and sixties."

"She can be frightful when she's on a mission," Juliet said to Bianca, the love she felt for Miranda obvious in her green eyes as she watched their oldest sister march away. "Miranda might not like to leave the house, but she sure can wield her power inside the perimeters of this property."

Bianca laughed at that, then caught the eye of Leo Santiago again. He smiled at her, waved a hand.

Juliet caught the exchange. "Bianca, I think you have an admirer."

Bianca shook her head. "I've known Leo for years. He's just being friendly." She blushed one more time as she turned away to greet her aunt. "Aunt Winnie, happy birthday. You sure don't look sixty."

"I did teach you manners, but you don't have to stretch things." Winifred Blanchard looked up at Bianca with a beaming smile. "Bianca, I'm so glad you're home."

The older woman got up to hug Bianca, surrounding her in the spicy scent of Shalimar her aunt had always worn. That scent brought back acute memories of her mother, Trudy. Aunt Winnie's spicy scent had always been in competition with her mother's softer, rose-scented perfume. How she missed the latter.

Pushing the shadows away, Bianca kissed her aunt. "You look lovely, and that's not a stretch."

"I look old," Aunt Winnie said, one bejeweled hand going to her severe chignon. "I've got more gray than red in my hair these days. But I guess I can't complain. It is so good to see you, darling."

"It's nice to be here," Bianca said, wishing she felt more comfortable in the manor. But it was good to feel the warmth of her sisters and her aunt, in spite of everything. "You have a crowd of well-wishers tonight."

Winnie grinned. "Yes, your father invited the whole town, I think."

"Everyone loves you," Bianca said. "This town owes you a lot."

"It's my home," Winnie said. Then she leaned close. "Let's get together and catch up later, when everyone's gone, okay, darling?"

"Okay," Bianca said, winking at her aunt. "It's a date."

Aunt Winnie had always held the family together, Bianca thought as she headed to the refreshment table set up in the corner of the big, antiqued-filled parlor. In fact, their aunt's eternal optimism and deep, abiding faith had been the glue that had kept the girls together after their mother's death. She remembered loving arms holding her close when they'd first arrived at Blanchard Manor. She remembered nightmares and screams, and all of the sisters, so young, so afraid, squeezing into Aunt Winnie's big bed late at night.

Aunt Winnie was like the princess in the tower. She'd never married, and for as long as Bianca could remember, Winnie had always lived in one wing of the big house, in her own private apartment, complete with a sitting room, a sun porch with a stunning view of the sea below, and a small library that held volumes of everything from Shakespeare to Maya Angelou. They'd often taken tea out on the sun porch, or at the big oak table centered in the library, safe and shut away from all their fears and horrors. Aunt Winnie had made life bearable for the girls, had distracted them by allowing them to be children.

And all the while, the sisters had mourned Trudy's death in a kind of screaming silence that whispered all around the big old house. No mention of Trudy was allowed unless they were alone with Aunt Winnie.

Bianca tried to stop the memories with practiced precision as she waited for the bartender to pour her a ginger ale, but the shadows came closer, moving over her as she remembered the night her mother had died in another such house not far from this one.

Rain and wind, voices shouting, the dark house groaning and creaking as lightning and thunder roared through the night. They had lived in their own place then, but vivid memories didn't mind taking up residence, no matter where one lived, Bianca reasoned. Even her tiny Victorian brownstone back in Boston's Beacon Hill neighborhood seemed to close in on her at times. She didn't like storms; didn't want to hear the thunder or the wind. And she refused to think about that night now.

Turning with her drink, Bianca was met with a broad chest. Her eyes traveled from the dark suit up to the man wearing it, her heart stopping.

"Hello, Bianca."

"Leo. It's…good to see you."

"Good to see you, too. I've been trying to work my way across the room since you came in the door."

"It's a bit crowded in here."

He leaned against the makeshift bar. "Sure is. Everybody who's anybody is here, I think."

Bianca took a sip of her soda, letting the tingling amber liquid slid down her parched throat. "Did you come for fun or out of duty?"

"Ouch," Leo said, his blue eyes twinkling. "That hurt."

"Oh, c'mon now, we both know you're a sworn

workaholic. You only show up at these things for one reason."

He lifted a dark eyebrow. "Oh, and what might that one reason be?"

She tilted her head and grinned. "Networking, my friend. You're always working that angle."

He tilted his head right back at her. "You know me too well."

Bianca wanted to say, no, she didn't really know him at all, but it felt good to be able to just…chat with someone and not feel threatened.

Until she saw the look in his eyes. Leo was looking at her with a renewed interest, as if he had only just now noticed her at all.

"What?" she asked, used to being direct in spite of her shyness.

"Nothing," he said with a shrug. "It's just that…well, it's good to see you, Bianca."

"Is it now?"

"You don't believe me?"

She shrugged. "Like I said, it takes one to know one."

"Did you say that?"

"I was thinking it."

"You don't have a very high opinion of me, do you?"

She studied him, causing him to be the first to look away this time. "I don't know everything about you, Leo. But I do know how demanding my father is. He only hires the best. And that means cutthroat, ruthless, determined and brilliant."

He looked surprised, and maybe a bit embarrassed. "Wow, it does take one to know one. I might say the same about you."

Bianca didn't know whether to be flattered or shocked. "I'm a lawyer. We don't get paid to be nice." Then she gave an eloquent shrug. "And Shakespeare said, 'First, we kill all the lawyers.'"

"What is it with you Blanchard women and Shakespeare? You all quote the Bard." He grinned and crunched some ice from his own drink. "So how is life as a big-time corporate lawyer in Boston anyway?"

"Life is pretty good," she said, meaning it. "I just finished a very important case—"

"Lewis verses Tatum, right?"

"Right," she said, impressed that he even knew about it.

"Lewis was a big technology gun, trying to imply that Tatum's smaller, less profitable company was slowly eating into their profits by undercutting their prices to clients, but Tatum had the might of right on his side. And you, of course. You proved that Tatum was an honest, hardworking man just trying to make a decent living. No funny business, except maybe on the side of Lewis, who might have withheld taxes on certain properties from the federal government and squandered huge amounts of the company's money on his own lavish lifestyle, which you so gently pointed out in your thorough research of the situation."

"That I did," she laughed, relaxing a little bit. "Leo, I didn't know you had such a fascination with corporate law."

He leaned close again. "Not so much a fascination with corporate law, as more of a fascination with one very pretty corporate lawyer from Boston."

"Uh-huh," Bianca said, looking away, her heart pounding. "I see."

"I hope you do," he said. Then he lifted his glass of mineral water to her in a salute, his gaze moving over her face. "I sincerely hope you do."

Bianca felt a new kind of warning move up and down her spine. But this one had nothing to do with Blanchard Manor or her dark memories. No, this delicious prickling of awareness was new and refreshing and completely different from anything she'd ever experienced. And it had everything to do with the man standing in front of her.

TWO

Bianca didn't know how to respond to Leo's words. He studied her with an almost predatory sort of longing. "It was nice to see you again, Leo," she said, placing her ginger ale down on the bar, then turning to walk away.

Leo's arm shot up to halt her. "I didn't mean to upset you."

His warm hand on her skin sent that little current of awareness running through Bianca's veins all over again. "Do I look upset?"

His eyes held hers. "Not really, more like confused. And formidable."

"I guess I can be both at times. Right now, however, I'm very clear on one thing. I'm not your type, so why are you flirting with me?"

"I thought that's what we always do on the rare occasions when our paths cross, flirt with each other."

She had to smile at that. "I'm afraid *I'm* not very

good at that particular art. I'm not well versed in the social graces."

"You don't even realize how good you are," he said, the words warm and sincere.

"Okay, what do you *really* want?" she asked, smelling a setup when she saw one.

He looked shocked, then embarrassed. "You figured me out already. I admit it. I'm trying to win points with the boss's daughter."

She laughed at that, appreciating his candidness. "Well, you have five other chances besides me. All of my sisters are here tonight."

"I'm not interested in your sisters," he said, turning super-serious with a lightning-quick clarity. "Only you."

At a loss for words, Bianca stood there staring up at him. She'd never realized how tall and broad shouldered the man was. Maybe because, even though they'd talked at other such functions, she'd never been this close to him before. He was just inches from her, his nearness causing little currents of energy to rush like sparklers throughout her system. It was very disturbing, in a nice, warm kind of way.

"Does that surprise you?" he asked, smiling down at her with an intensity that caused her heart to flutter.

"Well, yes. Coming out of the blue—"

"It's been here," he said, holding a hand to his heart, "for a very long time."

Before Bianca could answer, her father and his latest girlfriend, Alannah Stafford, walked up. Ronald Blanchard nodded with approval toward Leo, then smiled down at Bianca while Alannah gave them both a cool, condescending assessment.

"Bianca!" Ronald embraced her for a brief moment.

"Hello, Father." Forcing her attention away from Leo, Bianca glanced over her father's shoulder toward the elegant redhead at his side. She instantly noticed the glittering diamond necklace around Alannah's neck. Maybe because Alannah was deliberately fingering it with unsuppressed glee.

Backing away to stare up at her father, Bianca tried to concentrate on his debonair good looks. Ronald had aged, but with his silver-tinged dark hair and onyx eyes, he still had the kind of dignified bearing that caused women to turn their heads. First, for his handsome features, and second, for his wealth. Which brought Bianca back to Alannah.

"You look great," Bianca said to Ronald, smiling in spite of the knot in her stomach. "I guess we owe that to you, Alannah."

"I try to treat him right," Alannah said, her smile practiced and tight, her lips pouty and wide. Her overly colored hair shimmered and curled around her carefully plucked eyebrows, but her whole expression looked plastic.

Probably because of the Botox, Bianca thought, then asked God to forgive her for that catty thought.

"Isn't she amazing?" Ronald asked, his eyes sweeping over Alannah as he held the redhead close. "Honey, show Bianca your new necklace."

Alannah fingered the brilliant diamond-encrusted necklace. "Isn't it just the sweetest thing?"

"Sweet" wasn't exactly the word that came to Bianca's mind. More like "lavish" and "overblown." A flash of memory stabbed at her. She saw her mother, sitting at her vanity table, putting on a dainty necklace that held one perfect solitaire diamond.

Pushing that poignant memory away, Bianca said, "I thought Christmas was over." Then she noticed Leo still standing nearby, his expression bordering on amused as he heard her curt words.

"Not with your daddy," Alannah purred, her arm holding Ronald's with a possessive grip that caused her slinky green dress to twist around her curves. "He's like Santa Claus."

"That's so nice," Bianca said, giving her father a stern look. "He did always like to spoil all of us."

Ronald seemed to challenge that look. He smiled and practically dared Bianca to say anything else. "I tried, but if I recall, you wouldn't let me spoil you. Too stubborn and set in your ways."

Bianca wanted to ask if she'd gotten that particular trait from him or their mother, but refrained for the sake of politeness. She wouldn't ruin Aunt Winnie's special night by picking a fight with her father.

"How's everyone here?"

Bianca saw her father's executive assistant, Barbara Sanchez, out of the corner of her eye. Grateful for the interruption, she turned to face Barbara. "Hello, Barbara. How are you?"

"I'm doing just fine," Barbara said, her disapproving regard fluttering over Alannah. She placed an arm around Bianca's waist and tugged her close. "Just fine. How about you?"

"Couldn't be better," Bianca said, understanding passing between her and the loyal secretary as they smiled at each other. "How are your children?"

Alannah put a hand in the air, her long painted nails sparkling a deep pink. "Ronald, I've heard all of this before. Can we find something to drink?"

"Sure, honey." Ronald waved to Bianca, shook Leo's hand and gave him a wink, then turned to leave.

"Always pleasant," Barbara said, the hiss of her words echoing after the happy couple. She pushed at a strand of her shiny, smooth black hair, watching Alannah and Ronald.

"How do you tolerate her?" Bianca asked, then remembered Leo was there. "I'm sorry. I shouldn't have—"

Leo held up a hand. "I didn't hear a thing."

Barbara wagged her finger in his face. "And it had better stay that way."

"Yes, ma'am," Leo said, a wry smile on his face as his gaze danced from Barbara to Bianca. Then he grabbed Bianca's hand. "How about a walk on the bluffs, just to get some fresh air?"

Bianca looked at Barbara. Barbara shrugged and said, "Go on. It won't hurt. I'm sure the view is much better out there, anyway."

"I guess I've been here long enough to register an appropriate appearance," Bianca said. She turned to Leo. "Let me get my cloak."

"I'll go with you," he replied, already pulling her through the crowd. Then Bianca saw her father motioning to Leo.

"Your boss looks anxious," Bianca said, wondering why her father seemed so intent on getting Leo's attention. Probably wanted to warn him to stay away from the Blanchard girls. Ronald was nothing if not possessive, even with his wayward daughters.

Leo let out a sigh, then nodded toward Ronald. Turning back to Bianca, he said, "I'll meet you out on the terrace."

"Okay," Bianca replied, watching as he hurried to her father's side. "As usual, business always comes before pleasure around here," she muttered darkly to herself.

Leo didn't want to talk business with his boss right now. In fact, he didn't want to face Ronald Blanchard at all. But he knew if he didn't at least see what Mr. Blanchard wanted, he'd pay for it back at work on Monday morning. He loved the challenge of his job but sometimes had a huge distaste for the way his boss manipulated people. Just as he was trying to do with Leo now.

"Sir, you wanted to speak with me?" Leo asked in a hushed voice, anxious to be on his way with Bianca.

Ronald disengaged himself from the clinging redhead and pulled Leo close with one hand, strolling with him to a dark corner of the crowded room. "So I see you've made the first move toward Bianca. Very good, Leo. You always were a smooth talker."

Leo cringed but nodded. "I like Bianca. It's not that hard to strike up a conversation with her."

Ronald lifted his dark eyebrows. "That girl only wants to discuss court cases. I'm surprised she didn't bore you with all her legalese."

Wanting to defend Bianca, Leo said, "Actually, I find anything Bianca has to say very interesting, sir. We talked about a lot of things. You might try that yourself."

Ronald's expression went from patronizing to frowning. "*I* call the shots here. You'd best remember that. And you might want to remember who pays your salary. Now, I gave you a job to do—bring my daughter back to Stoneley and to Blanchard Fabrics. I need a good corporate lawyer and Bianca certainly fills the bill."

Leo nodded and let out a resolved sigh. "I agree,

sir, but Bianca plays by the book. If you're looking for her to break the law—"

Ronald looked affronted. "Have I ever suggested that?"

Leo couldn't nail him on that, but the implications were certainly there, based on Ronald's definite lack of scruples in how he dealt with people. "No, sir. I know you don't expect Bianca to do anything underhanded." *That would be my job,* he thought, a surprising resentment pooling inside his stomach. "Listen," he said to Ronald, "I'm not so sure I can do this. I don't want to hurt Bianca."

Ronald grabbed Leo's jacket sleeve. "Am I reading you right, Santiago? Do you have a thing for my daughter?"

Leo shrugged. "I told you, I like her. I *don't* like playing her. Bianca's a smart woman. I think she'll figure it out if I push too hard."

"And I told you, I pay your huge salary," Ronald countered, his voice rising just enough to make a few people standing nearby lift their heads. Lowering his voice to a stern whisper, he said, "I expect you to earn that salary by wooing my daughter back into the fold, without getting yourself all tangled in some misguided sense of honor and duty. You don't have to fall for her, Leo. Just make her think you have."

Leo stared over at the man he'd always admired and respected up until now. He'd done everything in his power over the past few years to get to his position as second-in-command at Blanchard Fabrics. But he'd never realized he might have lost both his morality and conscience in doing so.

He pushed away from Ronald and, without a word, stalked toward the back of the huge house. He needed that fresh air now more than ever. And he really needed to see Bianca again, but not for the reasons her father had ordered.

Bianca stood on the wide windblown terrace at the back of the mansion, her cloak drawn around her neck, the wind whipping her hair out of its chignon as she surveyed the dark, stormy sea below. A flurry of fresh snowflakes danced around her, reminding her that January in Maine could be very cruel.

Would Leo come and find her? Or would her father nip that in the bud before he even had a chance?

She tried not to be resentful, but that particular emotion always came to the surface, like the foam spraying up from the Atlantic, each time she came home to Blanchard Manor. She missed her mother, missed what might have been, missed being with her sisters and her aunt. And she mostly missed having a loving, caring, concerned father.

She felt safe and secure in her cozy little row house in Boston, safe and secure in her job at the prestigious law firm that had hired her straight out of law school. So why was it that all of her carefully masked insecurities always rose to the surface like flotsam from a shipwreck each time she came back here?

Maybe because since her mother's death all those years ago, they'd all been set adrift in doubt and confusion. Bianca held her arms around her middle, chilled to the bone as she recalled that dark night again. She'd just turned nine, and her mother had given birth to Juliet only a few months earlier. Her mother had been moody and sad—or that's at least how Bianca's nine-year-old mind had seen her mother back then. Now, Bianca and her sisters understood that their mother was probably suffering from postpartum depression.

Trudy would cry and cling to her five older daughters, then she'd sleep for hours on end, sometimes forgetting to feed baby Juliet until the nanny woke her.

Bianca remembered a terrible thunderstorm roaring over the ocean. She remembered hearing her parents arguing downstairs in the parlor. She could still feel Miranda's hand on hers as they'd stood at the top of the stairs, listening, their breaths coming faster and faster as the fight escalated. With the door to the downstairs parlor shut, they couldn't make out the words—just the loud, angry tones and muffled shouts.

"Be quiet," Miranda had told her, a finger to her lips. "We don't want to get in trouble."

Later, they'd heard footsteps coming up the expansive stairs and they'd run together back to their big bedroom to burrow underneath the heavy comforters on their matching twin beds. Then Trudy had come into their room, tears on her face as she kissed them good-night.

"What's wrong, Mommy?" Bianca had asked. "Did Daddy make you sad again?"

Trudy had shuddered, her cold hand stroking Bianca's face. "Hush, baby. I'm all right. Nothing for you to worry about. You need to go to sleep now. Everything will be okay in the morning."

Bianca often wondered what had really happened between her parents that night. This was the mystery that had shrouded all of them since her mother's death. Trudy had died that night, in a horrible accident when her car had gone off a cliff not far from the house. And all of her secrets had died with her.

The next morning, Ronald had gathered the girls together to explain that Trudy had packed her bags and driven away from her family in the middle of the terrible storm. And that she'd had a wreck. Their mother was dead.

"I'm so sorry, girls," he'd said, his voice shaking with emotion. "I begged her to not to go, not to abandon her family. But she wouldn't listen. She wouldn't listen. It's just us now. Your mother is gone now. Gone for good."

But never forgotten. Never forgotten, Bianca thought, tears forming in her eyes as the harsh wind howled around her.

"'To sleep, perchance to dream.'"

She heard those softly spoken words now as if her mother were standing here, whispering them in her ear. And remembered Trudy repeating that quote from Shakespeare over and over before she'd left their room. Had their disturbed mother been trying to tell them something that night?

So many questions, so much pain. A few days later, Ronald had brought his girls here to Blanchard Manor and they'd never again set foot in the house they'd shared with their mother. Ronald had ordered them to never mention Trudy's name in his presence. Except for a few smuggled photographs and mementos Bianca had hidden in a box in the attic, there was no trace of her mother. Thank goodness for Aunt Winnie. During those nights when the girls would all gather in her bed, she'd talk to them about Trudy and try to answers all of their many questions.

"Your mother loved each of you so much," Aunt Winnie would say over and over. "You have to remember that. She loved you all."

To this day, Bianca and her sisters savored these secret conversations, clinging to them just as they continued to cling to the hidden photographs, and to the whisper of Trudy's soft, bittersweet final words.

Lost in thought, Bianca felt a hand on her arm and jumped, turning with a gasp. "Leo!"

"I'm sorry," he said, holding her shoulders to steady her. "I didn't mean to scare you."

"I'm all right." Bianca glanced around, an eerie feeling descending on her there in the muted darkness. The shadows seemed to be leaping out at her. "It's just…this place holds a lot of bad memories for me."

Leo nodded toward the house. "It's a big, creepy place, that's for sure."

Bianca faced the mansion looming up behind them, the soft muted lights from the many rooms glowing like beacons in the cloudy night. The back of the house was covered in various porches and terraces, with stairs leading here, there and everywhere. It was even rumored there were secret caves hidden beneath the old house. "This house has always been forlorn and sad, in spite of Aunt Winnie's attempts to brighten it."

"She's an amazing woman."

Bianca appreciated the sincerity in his words. "Yes, Aunt Winnie is our rock. She's devout and faithful and full of a gracious spirit, which she's tried very hard to instill in all of us."

"I believe that," Leo said. "I can see that spirit in you."

Bianca couldn't stop the shiver of apprehension moving down her spine. "I haven't quite lived up to her expectations in the faith department."

"I think I could do better in that area myself," Leo replied, his gaze moving out over the ocean. "But you know how it is. You get caught up in work and forget all about your spiritual well-being. Work consumes you. It's all about making it to the top. Everything else gets shut out, even God's love and forgiveness."

Surprised that Leo even had a spiritual side, and not knowing how to respond to that, Bianca shivered again. "Brrr. It's cold out here."

He leaned close, then lifted his head to look up at the dark sky. "Sorry. Guess I got a little carried away. It's just been a long day."

"It's all right," Bianca said, trying to sound light. "You do work for my father, after all. He demands that kind of devotion." Then she tugged at his coat sleeve. "Don't let him...don't let him take all of you, though, Leo."

Leo pulled her cloak back around her, his eyes fixed on her face, the expression in his blue eyes as dark and unreadable as the sky, then he tugged her toward the steps. "Let's get out of here."

"Good idea." But as he guided her down the rocky, jagged steps toward the cliffs and the sea beyond, Bianca had to wonder if this was such a good idea, after all.

THREE

"Is this better?"

Bianca smiled over at Leo, then took a sip of the hot cocoa he'd ordered from the kitchen as they passed by on their way to the beach below the house. "Much better," she said. "I'm very impressed with how you ordered that poor busboy to find some hot cocoa and ASAP." Then she laughed. "But I'm even more impressed with how you climbed up that slope to get to the back door of the kitchen."

"I can be forceful when I want," Leo replied, holding his own mug of the steamy mixture up to his lips. "And I've been known to do a little rock climbing here and there, too."

"Both admirable traits for helping a damsel in distress."

"You look like you can take care of yourself," he replied, his grin splitting his face and showing off his white teeth in the moonless night.

Bianca let out sigh, glad that his earlier somber

mood had lifted. "I put on a good show. Practice makes perfect."

They were sitting in a big wooden swing someone had erected down on the beach long ago. This swing had been here as long as Bianca could remember, and it had been repaired and re-erected through storms, salty sea air, and constantly shifting sand.

She supposed she should take a hint from this rickety old swing. It had survived. Her faith probably needed just such an overhaul—a little repairing and a new resurrection. She'd been through a lot of wear and tear. Aunt Winnie had tried to teach Bianca and her sisters that God was always there, through storms and calm seas alike, but Bianca had pushed her spiritual nurturing away for too long now, just as Leo had described. Is that what he'd done, too?

Being here tonight, with Leo beside her, made Bianca long for some sort of centering, an anchor to hold her steady. She hadn't felt such a need in a long time, but now she ached for peace and contentment, and answers.

Leo glanced over at her. "I'm glad you're home. And I do think you can handle just about any situation."

A nearby yellow flame fluttered and hovered inside a glass-encased lamppost situated beyond the carved-out steps of the cliffs, giving off just enough brightness for them to see each other and their immediate surroundings.

"I wonder at that sometimes," she said in answer to his compliment. "I do take care of myself back in Boston. But here, I revert back into that lost, little girl."

Leo leaned forward, causing the swing to creak. "It must have been tough, losing your mother like that. I mean, it was so sudden."

Bianca finished her cocoa, then set the mug down in the damp sand at their feet. "It was terrible. We've all suffered in some way because of it. Miranda has this phobia about leaving the house, Juliet is the constant wanderer, unable to settle in one spot, Delia traveled across the world to Hawaii and gave up snowboarding to take up surfing of all things, just to get away, and Portia and Rissa stay hidden in the crowds of the New York art world, expressing themselves through pictures and stories—"

She stopped, put a hand to her mouth. "I'm sorry. I didn't mean to give you a rundown of our dysfunctions."

"I don't mind. But you left out yourself. How…how did her death affect you?"

She went silent for a minute, afraid to tell him all her fears. But something about seeing him again tonight, and maybe the way he'd been so attentive, had given her courage. "I'm the one with questions," she said on a low whisper. "Questions that don't have any answers, because we're not allowed to ask them." She glanced back up toward the house.

"We don't speak of my mother around here." Then she shrugged. "So I get answers for other people through my work. It's a vicarious way to bring myself some sense of peace, but it's never enough."

Wanting to change the suddenly intense mood, she tossed back her head. "All this melodrama. I'm such a downer, huh?"

Leo rocked the swing with a foot in the sand, his wool overcoat warm against Bianca's heavy cloak. "I told you, I don't mind. I've always been curious, you know, about what happened with your mother. Especially since she was a good friend of *my* mother's."

Bianca sat up to stare over at him. "That's right. I'd forgotten they were college roommates. Aunt Winnie had mentioned that. And I apologize again. I haven't even asked about your mother. How is she?"

Leo dropped his empty cup into the sand, where it landed with a soft thud. He looked at Bianca, the darkness of the night mirrored in his blue eyes. "She died almost three months ago."

Bianca's shock must have registered on her face. She could tell by Leo's expression that this was still a painful subject. "I'm so sorry. We had all heard about her illness, but I had hoped—" She stopped, regret coloring her next words. "I guess I haven't done a very good job of keeping up with things around here. No one told me about your mother's death."

"It's okay." He lowered his head. "I haven't talked about it with many people, but…*you* sure know how it feels. So I don't mind telling you it's been rough. My dad's been taking it hard and…I don't have the right words—"

"Do you blame God?"

He looked surprised, then thoughtful. "I did at first. But my dad told me not to do that. Even in his grief, he believes this is part of God's plan. And he believes my mother is safely in God's arms now, no matter how much we miss her." He shrugged, tugged at his coat. "I've never told anyone that. I mean, this isn't easy to talk about."

Bianca turned and, in a rare impulsive move, pulled him into her arms, hugging him tight. "Then talk to me. I *do* understand."

Leo held her close, his big hands going around her waist. "Thanks."

Bianca felt the warmth flowing from his touch all the way to her freezing toes. She pulled back, staring at him only to find the same surprise mirrored in his eyes. Had he felt that jolt of electricity, too? Apparently, he had. He touched a hand to her windblown hair, gently tucking a few strands behind her ear. Then he abruptly pulled away. "I have something to give you."

"Okay." An awkward awareness simmered between them as she waited for him to dig whatever it was out of the inside pocket of his coat.

He held the shining-white flat object out for her to see. "It's a picture of our mothers together. I found it when we were going through my mother's things. I wanted you to have it."

Bianca gasped, then took the picture. Barely able to see it, she got up to get closer to the gaslight.

Trudy's smile was just as Bianca remembered, a bit shy, a bit restrained, and almost bittersweet. She and Leo's mother were sitting on a bench in front of a big house, their arms together. Her mother's long blond hair was loose and flying in the wind. She looked so radiant, in spite of the frailness that surrounded her.

"Oh, Leo," Bianca said over her shoulder. She held a hand to her mouth, swallowing back tears. "Thank you."

Leo came to stand beside her, one hand touching her back. "It must have been taken long ago. It's at our beach house on Cape Cod. They both look so young and happy."

"They sure do," Bianca said, turning around to hug him again. "I can't tell you how much this means to me."

Leo held her close, then lifted her head with a hand underneath her chin. "I can see that in your eyes." Then he asked, "Do you still cry when you think about her?"

Bianca nodded and bit back tears. "Always."

He pulled her close again. "Me, too," he said. "Me, too. I sure miss my mother." He held Bianca there, his warmth and strength moving over her as their shared grief forged a gentle understanding between them. Then he pulled away, coughing lightly. "But if you tell anyone I cried on your shoulder, I'll deny it."

Sensing the teasing note in his words, Bianca smiled up at him. "Same here. We have to hang tough, right?"

He touched a hand to her face again. "Right." Then he pointed up toward the house. "In front of them, at least."

"But not with each other, okay?" she asked, meaning it. "Leo, if you ever need me—"

"I know where to find you," he finished, a finger soft against her lips. "And the same goes for me."

Bianca got the impression that their time here together had cost him. She could see the restraint in his eyes. He'd shown her his emotions, something she was sure he didn't like to do at all.

But then, nether did she, she reminded herself.

Leo opened the terrace doors for Bianca, his heart heavy with deception and betrayal. "Lunch tomorrow, remember?" They'd talked about that on the way back to the house.

"I won't forget," she said, nodding, her cheeks flushed from the cold, her eyes bright with hope and possibilities.

Leo's guilt heated his insides, making him wish he'd never agreed to help Ronald win Bianca back to the company. What had he done? And how could he change it now that he'd already gotten himself into this tangle? After spending time with Bianca, he didn't mind the tangle so much. But he did hate the underhanded way he'd been forced to get closer to her. And he didn't like using a picture of their two mothers to win her over. But, he reminded himself, he'd never meant for the picture to be a pawn. That he had given to her with sincerity and sympathy. Only now, even that well-intended act seemed tainted with deception.

How ironic, he thought. When had he developed a conscience? Probably from the moment he'd looked into Bianca Blanchard's pretty brown eyes.

He watched now as Bianca shrugged at her cloak, then he reached for it. "Here, I'll take that back to the coat-check," he said, helping her out of it. Folding the thick velvet material over his arm, he stood back, her sweetly scented wrap engulfing him in warmth as he remembered holding her close down on the beach.

She was beautiful in an exotic, quiet way. He'd never noticed just how beautiful. Her face was heart shaped and porcelain pale; her eyes were big and brown and beguiling; her wide, pouty lips created the most brilliant smile. He didn't want to do anything to mar that hopeful smile he'd seen on her face tonight.

But it might be too late to change that now.

He turned, ready to say his goodbyes and get out of this crowded room, when a commotion on the stairs stopped him. There was a crash, then a door slammed followed by heavy footsteps. Glancing over at Bianca, he followed her gaze toward the landing above the central hallway.

A strained, shaky voice rang out. "Where is everyone?"

Bianca's grandfather, Howard Blanchard, stood at the top of the stairs, teetering barefoot, in wrinkled pajamas, his white hair sticking out around his head, his expression wild with fear and confusion.

"Peg? Where is my tea? I want my tea."

Bianca sent Leo a frightened look as she rushed toward the stairs, Juliet on her heels. "Grandfather, what are you doing out of bed?"

Howard glanced down at them as he stood dangerously close to the top step, a fist in the air. "I want my tea. Tell Sonya to bring me my tea right this minute!"

The few remaining guests came out into the hallway, Winnie and all of Bianca's sisters in front, everyone staring up in horror at the scene at the top of the stairs. Unsure what to do, Leo ran up the stairs toward where Bianca had stopped just below the old man.

Juliet pushed past Bianca. "Stay there, Grandfather. I'll help you back to bed."

Howard gasped and stepped back, his rheumy

old eyes bright with shock as he squinted toward Juliet. "Trudy? What are you doing here? Go away. Go away, I said! It's all your fault. You're going to destroy this family. I have to stop you!"

He lunged, causing Juliet to scream as she tried to keep him from falling. The old man grabbed at Juliet, struggling with her, pushing at her outstretched arms, his eyes wild with hatred and confusion.

Leo hurried past a shocked Bianca. He reached Howard and caught him just in time to keep the frail old man from toppling down the stairs with Juliet.

"Mr. Blanchard, let me help you back to bed," Leo said, taking Howard by the arm while Bianca steadied Juliet.

"No," Howard replied, his voice echoing through the hushed rooms. "Get away! I don't know you. I don't know you! Did *she* bring you here?" He pointed a bony finger at Juliet. "She's evil, that one. Trudy, you get away from me."

Leo held tight, fighting the man's superhuman strength as Howard pushed toward Juliet again. A woman in a nurse's uniform showed up behind Howard to take his other arm.

"Mr. Blanchard, Sonya is bringing your tea right now, sir. It's your favorite. Earl Grey."

"Huh?" Howard said, jerking his head toward the nurse. "Peg? Where did you go? I was all alone."

"I know, I know," the attractive nurse replied in a soothing voice. "I was just in the next room. It's all right now." She motioned to Leo to let go. "Let's get you back to bed."

The woman Leo recognized as the housekeeper named Sonya appeared from the upstairs hallway, a stern expression on her face. She took the arm Leo had just released, mouthing a *thank-you* to him. "Mr. Blanchard, you gave us a fright, taking off like that. You don't need to be out without your slippers. You'll catch a cold."

Howard turned like a reluctant child, but he looked over his shoulder, his glazed eyes centering on Juliet. "You keep away from me, Trudy. You hear me? You'll ruin this family."

Leo stepped down toward Bianca. "Are you all right?"

She managed to move her head in a nod. "Juliet?"

Juliet slumped onto a step, her face white with fear. "He thought I was Mother." She buried her face in her hands. "He thought I was Trudy."

Ronald rushed up the stairs to stare down at Juliet, obviously as shaken as the others. Instead of comforting Juliet, he turned to Bianca. "He gets confused. He didn't know what he was saying."

Juliet looked up, her green eyes brimming with tears. "What did he mean? What was he saying about Mother?"

Ronald looked as pale as Juliet, but he regained his composure as he stared down at her. "I told you, he doesn't know what he's saying."

Leo noticed the hurt expression on Juliet's face as she switched from Ronald's harsh frown to Bianca's more sympathetic look. "I don't understand."

"Get up," Ronald said, waving a hand at Juliet. "You're making a scene."

Juliet's hurt changed into anger. "Well, we wouldn't want that, now would we, Father?"

Ronald looked at her as if she'd struck him. Alannah marched up the stairs and tried to pull him away, but he brushed her hand off his shoulder, then turned back to Juliet, his voice low. "He's a sick old man. I can't explain—"

Leo watched as Bianca leaned over them. "Father, maybe we should send the rest of the guests home."

"Yes," Ronald said, running a hand through his thick hair. "I think that would be best." He motioned for Bianca to sit with Juliet, then stomped past Leo to go back down the stairs.

Leo listened as Ronald tried to explain away the entire incident. But the look on Bianca's face told him she wouldn't let this go so easily. He realized she had questions, lots of questions.

This would only add to those questions. And if he knew one thing about Bianca Blanchard, she wouldn't stop until she had some answers. As Leo watched Bianca and her sisters help guide Juliet up the stairs, he could tell from their confused looks that they all felt the same way. All of the Blanchard sisters would now want answers to those questions they had never been allowed to ask before.

"Gather around, girls," Aunt Winnie told them an hour later. The sisters, all in pajamas and lounge-wear now, did as she said, finding spots atop the mauve down comforter of Aunt Winnie's big, canopied bed.

Just like the old days, Bianca thought, her mind still reeling from the scene with her grandfather. It was obvious they were all still shaken, even their usually serene aunt.

Winnie glanced over to where Bianca sat at the foot of the bed. "Ah, now, don't look so sad. I know your grandfather upset all of you, but he's terribly sick." Then she turned to where Juliet reclined on a fluffy pillow beside her. "Juliet, you *do* look so much like your mother. He didn't know what he was saying. He has a hard time remembering anyone these days."

Portia pushed at her curly black hair. "Why did he hate our mother so much, Aunt Winnie?"

Beside her, her twin Nerissa, or Rissa, as she'd always been called, nodded her head. "I'd like to know that myself. I don't remember how Mother and Grandfather felt about each other, but what I saw tonight left me…unsettled. He called our mother evil."

Miranda handed out cups of tea, her eyes downcast. "He mentions her a lot these days. Half of what he says doesn't make a bit of sense. It's hard to see him like this."

"How so? What does he say about Mother?" Delia, whose full name was Cordelia, asked, her arms folded over her stomach as she lay flat across the bed.

Miranda shrugged. "Sometimes, he shouts out that he's so sorry, as if he wants to tell her something. He calls out for her, then he tells all of us to leave him alone. I think maybe he regrets that he didn't welcome her into the family when Daddy married her."

Delia tugged at the hem of her oversize sweatshirt. "I would think he doesn't remember her at all."

"*I* don't remember her," Juliet said, her voice low, her green eyes full of pain. "Everyone says I look like her, and I do—I've seen pictures. But I don't believe she was evil. And I can't imagine why Grandfather would say that."

"Your mother was a good woman. She loved each of you so much. You were her treasure, her life. You must remember that, my dear ones."

Aunt Winnie patted the heavy photo album on her lap. "Now, what happened tonight was unfortunate, but we gathered here to remember the good times, right? And I do so appreciate this beautiful album you all put together for me. I can't thank you enough."

Bianca caught Miranda's glance, and wondered if her older sister thought the same thing as she. Aunt Winnie always told them how much Trudy had loved them, and she often told exciting, happy stories of her own time with Trudy, but she never went into detail about what had gone wrong with their parents' marriage, or what had really happened the night Trudy had died. Was everyone in this house keeping a secret?

Remembering the picture she'd tucked inside the pocket of her robe to show the others, Bianca lifted her head. "I have something to share with everyone. Leo gave it to me earlier tonight."

"What is it?" Portia asked, her brown eyes sparkling. "I did notice Leo and you all cozy together. Interesting."

"We were just catching up," Bianca replied, hoping she didn't sound defensive. "His mother passed away not long ago. But I guess some of you already knew that."

Her sisters went silent at that, until Miranda said, "Well, what did he give you?"

Bianca pulled out the picture Leo had given her. "It's a picture of Mother and Mrs. Santiago."

Suddenly, everyone gathered around Bianca, the sisters passing the picture among them. Bianca watched their reactions—a mixture of joy and pain, their expressions going from smiling to bittersweet—just like her mother in the picture.

Then Juliet took the photo and gasped. "I'd forgotten how vivid our resemblance really is." Bianca watched as tears gathered in her sister's eyes. "It's uncanny."

Aunt Winnie nodded, then faced Juliet. "Now do you see what your grandfather saw tonight? No wonder you scared him."

"That still doesn't explain why he called Mother an evil woman," Bianca said, the old questions burning inside her brain.

Aunt Winnie took the picture, studying it while she unconsciously ran a hand over the images cast there. Then she turned it over, as if she couldn't bear to look at it. "Oh, my," she said, pointing to something written there on the back. "This can't be right."

"What is it?" Bianca asked, leaning forward. "It's dated."

Aunt Winnie frowned. "Yes, but according to this date, this picture was taken a week *after* your mother died."

"What?" Miranda grabbed the picture and examined the date. "There must be a mistake. Maybe Mrs. Santiago got the date mixed up."

"Probably so," Aunt Winnie said, her eyes connecting with Bianca's. "That has to be it."

The room fell silent, but Bianca didn't miss the questioning looks on her sisters' faces. And she couldn't shake the rush of confusion burning through her system like a warning.

What if Mrs. Santiago hadn't gotten the date wrong?

What if the secrets radiating through this big, old house were finally coming to light at long last?

FOUR

Early the next morning, Bianca stood in the dining room, dressed in jeans and a Fair Isle sweater, a cup of steaming hot tea in her hand. She had not slept well at all. Each muscle in her neck and shoulders seemed to be permanently twisted and knotted. She couldn't get the image of the photo Leo had given her out of her mind. Nor the fact that the date on the back seemed to be all wrong. She pulled the photo from her sweater pocket, staring down at her mother's face as if she might figure everything out simply by holding the image close. Now, after viewing it several times last night and over and over again this morning, she could see things she hadn't noticed at first. Her mother's smile seemed forced, and there were dark circles underneath her eyes. Trudy clutched her friend's arm as is she were afraid to let go, a kind of panic in her bright eyes.

"'To sleep, perchance to dream.'"

Why did Bianca keep remembering that particular quote? And why had her own dreams been so fitful and full of lost memories? She'd have to go up to Aunt Winnie's library later and pull out the worn volume of Shakespeare plays and reread *Hamlet.* Maybe something there in the verses would jog her memory. She didn't dare go into the main library on this floor. Her father might ask too many questions. Although she did have one burning question she intended to ask him.

She whirled as footsteps echoed across the hallway. "Father?"

Ronald jerked around, a frown marring his handsome face. "Bianca? I didn't see you there."

"Aren't you going to have some breakfast?" she asked, her stomach churning as she steeled herself for the conversation she'd been practicing inside her head all morning. She intended to argue her case, just as she did in court each day. But her father would be a tough witness.

Ronald pulled at his striped silk tie. "I'm supposed to meet Alannah in the village at the Clam Bake. Were you waiting for me?"

The Clam Bake Café on Blueberry Road was famous for its fabulous brunches. And Alannah was well aware of the type of crowd that gathered there on weekend mornings. Probably wanted to make sure everyone saw her new bauble. Putting aside her negative feelings for Alannah, Bianca nodded. "Yes,

I was. I don't want you to be late, but I have to talk to you about something."

Ronald looked impatient, but he quickly hid that particular feeling behind a tight smile. "I have a couple of minutes." Then he pulled out one of the Queen Anne chairs for Bianca. "Let's sit down."

Bianca sank back against the cool wood of the polished chair, watching as her father poured himself a cup of coffee from the silver urn sitting on the rococo revival sideboard. She didn't miss the way his hand seemed to shake. But he held the delicate china cup and saucer firmly as he sat down across from her.

The long table seemed to glow as morning sunlight, so bright and cheery after last night's snow, streamed through the cream-colored sheers covering the high bay windows. A sun ray settled across the mint-green brocade tablecloth. Bianca glanced from the polished silver centerpiece, still full of fresh flowers from last night's party, to find her father eyeing her with suspicion and curiosity. Both the same as she felt right now.

"We didn't get much time to visit last night," she said, hoping to soften her reason for wanting to talk to him. "It's good to see you."

Ronald drummed his fingers against the table. "You, too, Bianca. I hear you're going strong, winning cases left and right. My friends at Burns and Collins must be gloating over having such a sharp associate."

"I hope to make partner in a few years," Bianca retorted, trying not to bask in her father's rare praise. Ronald's praise usually came with zingers.

"I don't doubt that," he said, toasting her with his coffee cup. "But you'd get that promotion a lot quicker right here at Blanchard Fabrics. You'd be our head legal eagle. And the pay could easily surpass what you're making now in Boston."

Bianca put down her teacup. "Oh, that again."

"Yes, that again," Ronald said, his smile smug.

"I didn't wait down here to talk about my career, Daddy."

Ronald sipped his coffee. "No, I don't suppose you did." He waited, silent and calculating, for her to speak. Then he gave her a real smile. "You haven't called me Daddy since you were little."

"An old habit." Bianca pulled the photo out again. "I need to show you something. Leo gave me this last night." She held it for a minute, reluctant to even let her father see it.

Ronald looked surprised, his attention falling to where she held the picture away from him. "You two did seem awfully cozy. I should warn you off him."

Bianca waved a hand in the air. "You don't have to do that. I'm fully aware of Leo's reputation."

"I see." He looked doubtful, and smug again. "So what do you have for me?"

Bianca pushed the picture across the table,

watching her father's expression go from smug to pale in seconds.

"Where did you get this?"

"I told you, Leo gave it to me. He thought I'd want to have it. You know he lost his mother recently."

Ronald's paleness changed to a deep flush. "Of course I know his mother died. He does work for me. And you can be sure I will ask him why he gave you this." He didn't bother hiding his anger. "I don't want to see this. Why are you showing me this? What was Leo thinking?"

Bianca stood up, jarring the china cups on the table. "He gave me this because that's my mother in the picture. Or do you refuse to acknowledge that?"

Ronald threw the picture down as if he couldn't bear to touch it. "I can see clearly that…Trudy… That your mother is in the photo, Bianca. But Leo had no right, no right." He stood, too, his hands once again shaking.

"He had every right. We've both lost our mothers, and the grief never ends, really. He needed someone to talk to."

Ronald bobbed his head. "And he picked you."

Bianca watched, shocked, as her father bunched his fists at his sides, clutching them tightly against the crisp wool of his navy suit. He looked as if he'd been betrayed.

Maybe they all had.

"Father, what happened to Mother that night?"

Ronald grabbed onto the back of his chair. "I don't want to discuss this."

"But we need to," Bianca said, pushing just as she would if she were cross-examining, but her tone was gentle in spite of her need to know. "Because you see, the date on the back of this picture makes it seem as though it had been taken *after* my mother's death."

The shock on her father's face scared Bianca. She truly feared he was going to have a heart attack. He grabbed for the picture, staring first at the images there, then turning it to read the date written on the back. "It can't be," he said, shaking his head. "It's wrong. This is wrong. Leo is playing a cruel joke on you."

"Leo doesn't know about the date being inaccurate. I didn't mention it to him."

"But he has to know," Ronald insisted, banging his fist down. "He did this...deliberately."

"Why would Leo do that?" Bianca asked, that odd feeling of being watched moving down her spine again. "You're not making sense."

Ronald backed away, pushing a hand through his thick hair. "I'll tell you what makes sense, Bianca. Your mother is dead. She died the night she decided to leave me. That's the only thing that makes sense." He dropped his hands to his side. "I'm glad you're home, Bianca, and you know you are welcome to stay as long as you like, but I will *not* discuss this again."

Bianca started to tremble as she watched her

father stomp away. When she heard the slamming of his study door, she jumped. The big airy dining room suddenly felt cold and dreary, in spite of the morning sun.

Sonya came rushing in from the butler's pantry. "Is everything all right? I heard shouting—"

"It's fine," Bianca told the anxious housekeeper. "We didn't mean to disturb you, Sonya."

The housekeeper's dark eyes widened. "Did your father leave already?"

Bianca nodded as she sank down on a chair. "Yes, he had to go." She waved Sonya away. "I'm just going to finish my breakfast. I'll let you know if I need anything."

Juliet found her a few minutes later, staring down at the picture. "What happened?"

Bianca pointed to the picture, her eyes filling with unshed tears of frustration. "Father and I had a quarrel. He won't talk about her at all."

Juliet picked up the photo. "You showed this to him?"

"Yes, and pointed out the date."

"Oh, Bianca, you shouldn't have done that."

"And why not? It doesn't add up. If Mother truly was alive when this picture was dated, then nothing adds up. And it looks like Father's hiding something. I have to know the truth."

"Nothing has ever added up around here," Juliet said, her arms wrapped against her fashionable embroidered wool sweater coat. "But I can't bear you chasing after some false hope, based on a scribbled date from an old photograph. No wonder Father is so upset."

Bianca saw the pain in Juliet's eyes. She was wrong to even voice a hope to Juliet, she realized. Juliet blamed herself for her mother's death. She would be devastated if she thought Trudy might be alive, only to find out Bianca's suspicions were just dreams.

Dreams that somehow echoed the last thing her mother had said to her, Bianca thought. But she didn't voice that to Juliet. "You're right. I know it's crazy. But I had to ask, just to find out. I thought maybe he'd finally talk to me about her."

"Well, now you know. Our father isn't going to ever explain anything to us about Mother. We need to let her rest, let this rest."

Bianca nodded as Juliet turned to leave. "I'm sorry I upset you."

Juliet turned at the arched doorway. "You're upsetting yourself and everyone else. I wish Leo hadn't given you that picture." Then she came back to put her arms around Bianca's neck. "Just let it go and enjoy this time we have here together, please?"

Bianca held the picture close as her sister walked away, and remembered that her father had basically said almost the same thing, but in a much colder way. Which only brought up another question.

Why had Leo given *her* the photo?

* * *

Why had he ever agreed to this, Leo wondered as he sat in the Lighthouse restaurant on Ocean Drive, waiting for Bianca to meet him for lunch. He didn't mind lunch with her; that wasn't the problem.

The problem was the deal he'd made with Ronald Blanchard. Win Bianca over and convince her to come to work at Blanchard Fabrics. "Do this for me," Ronald had said, "and I won't have to make things tough for Bianca back in Boston."

Leo couldn't believe Ronald would stoop so low as to try to have his own daughter fired from her job. But the veiled threat had been there, right along with the same threat toward Leo if he didn't take on this assignment.

"'What a tangled web…'"

Leo groaned. Great, now he was quoting Shakespeare. Angry with himself, he looked out the wide window toward the ocean. The blue waters hissed and foamed against the craggy rocks just below the dining room of what had once been a real lighthouse. Outside, snow clung to the deck and the shrubs and rocks surrounding the parking lot. It was cold, but the sunshine and the big fire crackling in the massive stone fireplace across the room gave a hint of warmth to the afternoon.

Leo heard the door open and looked up. Bianca stood in the threshold, dressed in a tan leather coat and a cute striped wool hat and matching scarf. She waved and headed over when she saw him.

"Hi," he said, getting up to help her with her coat and scarf. "Nice day, huh?"

She nodded, fluffing the long dark hair that fell out from underneath her hat when she removed it. "Yes, especially after that snow last night. Things always seem so fresh and clear after new-fallen snow."

Leo pushed her chair in for her, then sat back down. "Then why do you have such a pained expression on your face? Do you regret agreeing to have lunch with me?"

She looked down at the white tablecloth covering the heavy wooden table. "No, it's not that." Raising her head, she looked straight at him. "I showed my father the picture you gave me. He was furious."

"Why? There's no crime in you having a picture of your mother, is there?"

A waitress came over, smiling down at them with big blue eyes. "Ready to order?"

Leo nodded toward Bianca. She glanced at the menu. "I'll have the clam chowder. And some hot tea."

"That sounds good to me, too," Leo said, smiling at the young waitress. "Except make my drink coffee."

"I'll bring some water out, too," the waitress said, giving Leo an appreciative smile. "How about some of our lobster rolls for starters? We just mixed the lobster salad fresh."

"Great," Leo replied, still smiling. "Nothing like a big old sandwich stuffed with chopped lobster."

"I'll bring some right out," the waitress said, grinning from ear to ear.

"Wow, you sure have a way with the ladies," Bianca said, her expression full of mirth as she watched the cute blonde sashay to the kitchen.

"It's my style." But Leo wanted to get back to Ronald and the picture. If Ronald was taking out his frustrations toward Leo on Bianca, that was a whole new ball game. "Now, what happened with your father?"

"Like I said, he got angry at me. Did you know the date on the back of the picture says it was taken a week *after* my mother died?"

Leo sat up straight. "What?"

"You didn't notice that?"

He shook his head. "I've never been sure of exactly when your mother passed away, so I guess the date had no relevance to me."

"Well, it does to me," Bianca replied, sounding slightly accusatory. "I had this idea that maybe you saw the discrepancy. At least that's what my father implied. He thinks you did this deliberately."

Leo's gut burned. Bianca had just verified what he'd suspected. Ronald would nail him against the wall with this one. "That I knew about the date and deliberately showed it to you? Bianca, why would

I be so thoughtless? If I'd known, I wouldn't have shown you the picture at all. I'm sorry I did now."

She shook her head, causing her thick hair to fall around her face. "No, I'm *glad* you did. I needed to see this." Leaning close, she said, "Leo, for as long as I can remember, I've had questions about my mother's death. Questions I didn't dare voice, even to my sisters. Now, I find a picture of her dated *after* she died? I have to find out why."

"I can call my dad," he offered, wanting to put any concerns out of her mind. "He might remember something."

Her eyes lit up. "That's a good idea."

The smiling waitress showed up with their water and a basket of buttered baguettes brimming with lobster salad.

Bianca waited until the girl left before continuing. "Maybe he can clarify things for us at least." Then she looked out toward the sea. "I'm thinking about hiring a private investigator, just to find out what I can."

"Regarding your mother?"

"Regarding my mother's *death.* Think about it—none of us has ever questioned our father's version of things. Maybe it's time one of us did."

Leo grabbed her hand. "Bianca, you're treading in dangerous territory. I know how grief can eat away at you, but you can't bring your mother back, especially not with an old photograph."

"A photograph that leaves me full of doubt and

questions," she retorted, her eyes wide. "It just verifies what I've wanted to do since I became a lawyer—find out the truth."

Leo let go of her hand. What had he created here? Ronald obviously already thought Leo had used the picture to get next to him. Bianca doubted his motives for even talking to her, let along giving her a mysterious picture, and now he'd set her on some sort of quest that could only lead to heartache down the road.

"Look," he said, whispering so no one could overhear. "It's just an old picture, and the date is probably wrong. I'm sorry it's dredged up so much pain for you and your family."

"All of my sisters saw the picture. Aunt Winnie noticed the date. It's too late to change that now."

"Maybe so, but it's not too late to just let this go. Leave it alone. I don't want to see you get hurt."

And he meant that. He'd started this deception. Now it would be up to him to make sure Bianca was safe and protected, from both her father's treachery and his.

"I can't be any more hurt than I've been for most of my life," Bianca said, glancing out at the ocean again. "Look at that water, Leo. It's so timeless, so sure. It's never-ending. I want that kind of peace. And I can't have that until I find the truth."

"What if you don't like what you find?"

She whirled to stare over at him. "I'll just have to deal with that when it comes." Shrugging, she lowered her voice. "I'm going to talk to an investigator this afternoon. Just for my own peace of mind."

"You've been thinking this through."

"All night long."

"Then I'm going with you."

"You don't have to do that."

"I insist. I got this started. I intend to follow through. And that means, I'm not letting you make a move without me. After we eat, I'll call my father, then we'll find a P.I. together."

"Rescuing me again?" At least asking that made her smile.

"I know you could deal with this all on your own, but look at it this way—you don't have to."

"But this could put a strain on things, with you and my father. He'll confront you, just wait."

An understatement, but Leo didn't say that out loud. "I'll take care of that, don't worry. Right now, I'm more concerned about the strain I see in your eyes. I want to help."

She lowered her eyes, shy again. "That's nice to hear, for a change."

Leo wondered just how much she did deal with, all alone in Boston. She didn't deserve the kind of deceit and treachery her father dished out on a regular basis. "Good, then it's settled."

"Okay." Her smile went soft and warm, then quickly changed into a frown. "I don't have too much time here. I only took a few days off from work, and I have a huge case coming up in about a month. I did bring some of the preliminary work with me, and I can at least do research through the Internet, but I want to spend as much time as possible on finding out the facts of my mother's death. We need some honest answers."

Leo took her hand again. "Stop worrying. And don't get your hopes up on this. You might just find out what you already know—that your mother died from a tragic accident."

She didn't respond to that. Instead, she simply sat there, her eyes dark and unreadable, her whole demeanor still and quiet. Leo wondered if this was how she became before she went to bat for her clients. She looked formidable, dangerous, ready to strike.

And very determined.

"Even if I verify that, at least maybe I can get the whole story, somehow. At least I can finally know that I tried to honor her death. She'd never been given that kind of honor. You know, even her funeral was strange. Father had her cremated. No casket, no viewing, nothing. Just a short ceremony and then an urn of ashes placed in the family vault. I barely remember anything about that, except that I hated the thought of our beautiful mother being cremated. Gone like dust."

Leo listened to her and saw the doubt and the determination on her face. And admired her even more. Bianca Blanchard was a strong, beautiful woman, and somehow, in spite of her father's coldness and secrets and her mother's awful death, she'd managed to remain true and good and honorable. As he watched her, he realized that Ronald Blanchard had at last made a fatal mistake.

He'd forced Leo and Bianca together, no matter how dubious his motives. The joke was on him now, because his plan was going to backfire and blow up right in his face.

Leo's loyalty had just shifted to a different Blanchard. It now belonged to the woman sitting across from him.

FIVE

"I'm sorry my father wasn't much help," Leo told Bianca when they pulled up to where she'd left her car at the restaurant. "He couldn't remember when your mother came to visit. Things are fuzzy for him these days."

"It's okay," Bianca said. Staring out at the azure-tinged ocean, she let out a long sigh. "At least we found a private investigator. I'll meet with Mr. McGraw again first thing in the morning, after I talk to Juliet. I have to make her understand—"

"Just be careful," Leo said, his gut burning. And it wasn't from the clam chowder. "McGraw looks shifty to me."

"Shifty?" She pushed at his arm. "That's a good way of describing him, I suppose."

He hadn't been that impressed with Garrett McGraw, but the slick, hard-edged P.I. was about the only game in town around here. And Bianca didn't want to waste time trying to locate someone else.

"Just make sure you stay on him. Don't let him take your money and then give you the runaround."

"I'll be fine," Bianca said, smiling. "Remember, I deal with these kind of people on a regular basis."

"I remember. But you need to remember I'm involved in this, too. And I won't stand by and let you get in trouble."

"Okay, all right." She opened the car door. "That's awfully sweet of you."

He didn't feel so sweet. He felt strange and off center. All of Leo's protective instincts suddenly kicked in. Bianca looked so young and pretty with her hair down and windblown. He had to remind himself that she'd been out on her own for several years now, and she was accustomed to handling things her way. "Just be careful."

"I promise," she said, nodding. "I've got to go. I want to spend some time with Aunt Winnie and my sisters before they leave. Maybe I can find out a little more about Mother if I get Aunt Winnie talking." She shook her head. "It's so sad that I'm thirty-two years old and I still don't know that much about my mother or her side of the family. It's as if when she died, all her history died with her. No wonder my sisters and I are still all single—we're too afraid of commitment, too afraid of getting hurt. If I can find some answers, maybe I can help my sisters to heal and get on with their lives, too."

"What about you?" Leo asked, thinking she could

use some tender loving care herself. Then he added a big *wow* to that thought. He'd never considered himself one for that kind of nurturing. But then, that was before Bianca had looked into his eyes.

"Me?" she asked, her eyes bright. "I just want to know the truth. The complete truth, good or bad."

Leo got out to come around to her side of the car, wondering how she'd react right now if he just blurted out his own truth to her. *Not now,* he thought. *Not when she's already dealing with this mystery surrounding her mother. Another time.* Holding the door for her, he said, "I enjoyed lunch."

Bianca gathered her purse and hat, then stepped into the brisk wind. Wrapping her scarf around her neck, she said, "But you didn't know you'd be out searching for a private investigator instead of getting dessert, right?"

"It was a rather different kind of date."

"Was that what it was—a date?"

He tilted his head, studying her face. "I think so. Am I allowed to call it that?"

She tugged her hat on, then shrugged. "You can call it whatever you want. I enjoyed it, and I do appreciate your help."

"Okay, then when can we have another one—date, that is?"

Her eyes widened. "You mean, I didn't scare you away with all this mystery and intrigue?"

He leaned close, the sound of the ocean humming

in his ears. Or maybe it was the sound of his pulse racing. "The mystery here is how…seeing you again has affected me."

She blushed and looked away. "I shouldn't be doing this. I shouldn't involve you in my troubles."

Leo pulled her around to face him again. "Hey, *I* gave you the picture, remember. Neither of us knew it would lead to so many questions." He held his hands on her shoulders. "But I'm glad it did lead to you and I getting to know each other better. I don't regret that at all."

"You might before this is over."

The look of firm resolve in her dark eyes scared him. How could he protect her if she went off on all these tangents without any backup? "Let's just take it one step at a time, okay? Don't do anything crazy. At least not without me there with you."

"Now that *does* sound like a fun date."

He laughed then, glad to see her soft smile return. "Well, once this is over, we'll have a real date, I promise."

"I'm going to hold you to that."

"Good." He gave her a quick peck on the cheek, then turned toward his car. "I'm late. Hope my boss hasn't noticed."

"I think he's noticed a lot," she called after him. "So you be careful yourself."

"Always." He got inside his black vintage Mercedes, then waited until she was safely in her own little silver Miata, waving to her as she backed up and pulled out of the parking lot. His thoughts still on Bianca, Leo backed up, too. But another car shot around the corner, causing Leo to slam on his brakes.

"Where's the fire?" he asked, shaking his head as the hooded driver zoomed by and headed in the same direction as Bianca. Glancing at his watch, Leo winced. "Actually I should be the one speeding. I'm late getting back to work."

And he had a certain feeling he was already in big trouble with the boss.

"Well, finally, I have all six of you together again," Aunt Winnie said at dinner that night. "Just the girls." She reached for the nearest two hands. "Let's say grace."

After Aunt Winnie asked God to bless the food and those eating the food, Bianca surveyed the table, listening as her sisters chattered and laughed. "So what did everyone do today?"

Miranda dipped up the steaming butternut squash, while Aunt Winnie watched with a serene expression as the stoic housekeeper Sonya served the grilled chicken. "I helped Sonya prepare this meal most of the afternoon," Miranda said, "but then Father decided to have dinner in town with Alannah."

"She couldn't handle dinner with all of us," Portia said, her chunky red bracelet clanking against the table.

Bianca thought, more like their father couldn't face them after his confrontation with her this morning. But she didn't tell her sisters that, and she didn't intend to tell them what she was about, either. Juliet was the only one who knew any of this, so Bianca wanted to update her. And the others had somehow pushed away the questions regarding the picture, just as they'd pushed away everything about their mother. "I wonder if Father will ever marry Alannah," she said now. Somehow she couldn't picture Ronald settling down with just one woman.

"It hasn't come up," Aunt Winnie said from her spot at the head of the table. "I don't know if my brother will ever marry again."

Bianca looked across the table at Juliet, and saw the shadows falling across her sister's face. She would have to find a way to get Juliet alone, to tell her about hiring Garrett McGraw. Juliet would probably be furious, but Bianca would handle that, somehow. They'd always been so close, so in tune with each other. Even when Juliet was off traipsing all over Europe, they'd stayed in touch. Bianca hoped that closeness wouldn't change, no matter what she found out about their mother.

"Where were you all day, Bianca?" Delia asked, a dinner roll in her hand.

"Oh, I went into the village—"

"And had lunch with Leo Santiago," Aunt Winnie said with a knowing smile. "How did that go?"

Bianca ignored the pointed interest her sisters suddenly seemed to be showing, but she didn't miss Juliet's frown. "It was fine. We ate at the Lighthouse."

"Mmm, good food, good ambience. Sounds almost like a date," Rissa said, tossing her dark curls away from her face.

"We had lunch, nothing more," Bianca retorted.

Miranda settled into her chair. "Well, I'd say it's high time one of us formed some sort of relationship with a man. Since I don't have any prospects, I'm happy for Bianca, at least."

"Maybe we're all like Father, commitment-shy," Delia retorted. She ran a hand over her short brown hair. "I did try once, but then we all know how that marriage ended. I don't want to go through that again."

Delia's dark eyes seemed bottomless as her expression changed from cheerful to regretful. Bianca's younger sister had secretly married her high-school sweetheart when she was seventeen. Of course, their father had had the marriage annulled, and Delia's groom had disappeared. Yet another thing from the past they didn't mention very often.

The room went quiet, but Aunt Winnie tried to gloss things over. "I think we all have a past love we think about now and then." Even she looked wistful for a minute. Then she said, "I just wish all of you could find someone to settle down with. None of us are getting any younger, and I worry about you."

"Well, don't worry about me. I'm not forming anything except friendship," Bianca said, her knife slicing into the tender rosemary-scented chicken. "I can't stay here long enough for anything more."

"And if you could stay?" Juliet asked, her eyes bright with interest and the dare that Bianca knew so well.

"I can't. End of discussion. I've got an important case coming up—Internet piracy, technological espionage, that sort of thing. It will require my full attention."

"'The lady doth protest too much methinks,'" Miranda said with a grin.

"I'm not protesting. Just trying to explain that there is nothing going on between Leo and me." Bianca glanced around the table, sure that none of her sisters believed her. So she tried changing the subject. "How's Grandfather today?"

Aunt Winnie put down her fork. "Same as usual. I visited with him this afternoon, but of course he didn't even know I was in the room."

"How did you get past Peg the Protector?" Rissa asked, her tone bored, in spite of the lift of her dark eyebrows.

"Peg knows to let me see my own father," Winnie said. "After all, I do pay the woman's salary."

"Does she live here now?" Bianca asked, curious as to how the nurse had gained so much power. Peg seemed to always be lurking about, but the attractive middle-aged nurse was highly trained, and she seemed to genuinely care about Grandfather Howard's welfare.

"Yes, she's here full-time now, in a room near Father's on the third floor," Aunt Winnie told them. "It became necessary when Father got worse this summer. He doesn't have long, I'm afraid. Peg needed to be close by."

"Peg is so devoted," Miranda whispered, checking to make sure they were alone. "She insists on watching over him without end. We have to *make* her take time off. Every now and then, she'll hurry into town on quick errands, but other than that, she rarely leaves his side."

"Admirable," Aunt Winnie replied, her smile hard to read.

"Very," Portia retorted, her tone leaving little doubt that she wasn't all that impressed with Peg.

Bianca felt a prickling sensation and turned to find the housekeeper, Sonya Garcia, standing just inside the butler's pantry. The look on the housekeeper's face before she stepped away gave Bianca the chills.

And made her wonder once again just how many secrets were hidden in this old house.

"This isn't much to work with."

Bianca looked across the oak desk at the man she'd hired to help her trace information about her mother. Garrett McGraw could only be described as seedy. Or shifty, as Leo had called him. The man was tall and painfully thin, with more hair growing on his goatee than on his shiny balding head. His brown eyes darted here and there, making Bianca think of a ferret.

Deciding beggars couldn't be choosers, she sat up in her chair. "I don't have much information, Mr. McGraw. That's why I'm hiring you. All I can tell you is that there is a possibility that my mother might be alive somewhere. We have to start there."

He tapped a finger on the photo in his hand. "Based on the date on this picture?"

Bianca nodded and cleared her throat. Why was this so hard? "That and a feeling I've had for a long time now. And my father's evasions. There are a lot of unanswered questions surrounding her death. I need you to research it thoroughly. That night, the accident, where the car wound up. And track down relatives. I don't know any of my mother's side of the family. And I have no idea where my maternal grandparents are, or if they're still alive."

Garrett scratched at what little hair he had on the back of his head. "Might take some time…and money."

"I don't have much time, so make this urgent, and you'll get a bonus for your extra time, of course."

He grinned wolfishly. “Of course.” Then he handed the picture back to her. “I’ll have to dig through police reports and courthouse records, and old newspapers. Then maybe ask around—”

“Be careful there,” Bianca cautioned. “I don’t want anyone else in the family or this town to know about this—especially my father.”

Garrett pushed back in his squeaky vinyl chair. “I’ll sure make a note of that. Don’t want to tangle with Ronald Blanchard.”

“No, you don’t,” Bianca replied, schooling her expression to show she meant it. “When can you get started?”

Garrett chuckled. “You’re in luck. I don’t have a heavy caseload right now.”

“Good,” Bianca said, thinking from the looks of his dusty, dirty office, he hadn’t had a case in a long time. “I’ll expect reports often. Don’t call Blanchard Manor. You can call the cell number I gave you, day or night.”

“Got it,” the investigator said, rising from his chair to walk her the short distance to the door.

Bianca thought she heard a shuffling sound as they stepped out into the hallway. “Were you expecting someone else?”

He looked at his watch. “Not today, no, ma’am. But there are a couple of other offices in this building, people always coming and going.”

“Funny, I thought I heard something—?”

"Might be those stray cats that hang around out back."

"Maybe."

She left through the outer door leading to the side street, the same sensation of being watched hitting her again. She thought about Sonya Garcia, wondering why the housekeeper had looked so hostile last night. But then, all the household staff at Blanchard Manor seemed stoic and stern, probably because Ronald Blanchard didn't mix and mingle in a friendly way with the hired help.

"Silly," she whispered as she headed to her car. "All this melodrama has you imagining things."

Then she felt the wind hitting her with a swish as a car came careening around the corner, headed right toward her. Backing up, she gasped and quickly edged around the front of her own vehicle just as the other car zoomed by.

"That was close."

The dark sedan had barely missed hitting her.

For a minute, Bianca couldn't move. She just stood there, staring after the car. Unable to see who'd been driving, she shrugged. "Stop this," she told herself as she got in her car. "Stop looking for those shadows everywhere."

But as she sat there, she could almost feel the old familiar shadows of her childhood bearing down on her.

Even in the bright light of day.

* * *

Leo looked up to find Ronald Blanchard standing in the doorway of his office. And the look on his face didn't bode well at all.

"Ronald, what can I do for you?"

Ronald entered the room, closing the heavy door behind him. "That's a very good question, Leo. First, you can explain what kind of game you're playing with my daughter."

"I don't know what you mean," Leo said, slapping shut the file he'd been studying about recycling scrap textiles into new, nontoxic fabrics. He'd had a sleepless night and a rough morning, so he wasn't in the mood for a lecture. "I thought you were the one playing games here."

Ronald leaned over the table, the rage in his eyes reminding Leo of just how much power the Blanchards held in Stoneley. This very building had been here for over a century, as old and timeless as the cliffs and the ocean beyond. The imposing factory out past the office building might have been overhauled and updated through the years, but the Blanchard Fabrics building was a one-hundred-year-old historical redbrick landmark that demanded respect. And so did its owners.

"Is this about our deal?" he asked Ronald, bracing for the onslaught of anger he could see coming.

"I don't think I've been clear with you, Leo," Ronald said, his teeth clenching with each word. "I never instructed you to dredge up the past and stir up trouble."

"If you're talking about the picture—"

"You know exactly what I'm talking about," Ronald interrupted, slamming a fist on the desk. "What were you thinking, giving Bianca a picture of her dead mother?"

Leo ran a hand down his face. "I never thought it would upset her."

"Or me? Did you think about how it would bother *me?*"

"No, not really. I just wanted her to have it."

"Well, that was the worst way you could get close to my daughter. Now she's asking questions, wanting to know things about her mother. I won't stand for it!"

Leo got up to roll his shirtsleeves down, giving Ronald a direct look as he buttoned each cuff. "Have you thought about being honest with Bianca? She just wants to know more about her mother. She's hurting—"

"Shut up." Ronald's face turned as red as the accent pillows on the cream leather sofa against the wall. "You have no business messing in this, Leo."

"You gave me permission to mess with your daughter, Mr. Blanchard. I can't help what happened."

"Yes, you can. If you value your job here, you'll leave Bianca alone."

"Oh, so now you're changing my orders?"

"Yes, I am. Just forget it, all of it. You've already caused enough trouble. If you can't stick to the original plan, then you might need to look elsewhere for employment."

Leo nodded, hating the way he'd betrayed Bianca. Now he was going to betray the man who'd talked him into doing it in the first place. "I understand, sir. I'm sorry about the picture. But I can't back away from Bianca now. She'd be even more suspicious."

He watched as Ronald's brain started spinning. And prayed his ploy would give Bianca some time. "Mr. Blanchard, let me handle Bianca. If you get defensive, she'll simply ask more questions. If I keep her occupied, maybe it will take her mind off her mother." He waited a minute, then added, "I had planned on taking her out to dinner later this week. I thought I could bring up the factory, tell her about things around here. If I cancel now, she might think you interfered. And that would make her even more unwilling to consider coming to work for Blanchard Fabrics."

Ronald put his hands on his hips, then stormed to the window behind Leo's desk. "Well, you've certainly got me there. I overreacted to the picture. It's just that seeing Trudy, so young, so beautiful…it left me unsettled."

Leo felt a pang of remorse. Maybe Ronald Blanchard did have a heart after all. "I'm sorry for your loss. I can't imagine what you've all been through. And I'm really sorry that I stirred that up. I'll try to smooth things over with Bianca." *And protect her from you.*

Ronald turned then, nodding, the tension leaving his face. "You've got one more chance, Leo. One more chance. I don't need Bianca angry at me. I need her happy, and wanting to come home. That's the plan. We both need to stick to the plan."

"I'll do my best, I promise."

Leo held his breath as Ronald stomped out of the room.

Then he put his head in his hands and let out a long sigh. "Lord, I'm in a mess here. I need help. I have to protect Bianca." He closed his eyes, wondering if he'd have the courage to tell her about his original intentions. Would she just laugh and tell him it was all right? Or would she be hurt and angry? Did she really need to hear this now? No, not yet. Deciding he'd explain to her after she got those answers she needed regarding her mother, Leo held to the one pledge he'd given to both Bianca and her father. He was going to protect her, no matter the consequences.

He just never imagined he'd wind up protecting her from her own father. But that was exactly what he had to do. And somehow, he had to do it without betraying either of them.

SIX

Bianca glanced around the tiny dining room of the out-of-the-way coffeehouse where she'd chosen to meet Garrett McGraw. It had been almost a week since she'd hired him, and she'd been sitting on pins and needles, wondering what he might find out. Now she was about to get a full report. If the man ever showed up.

Thinking back over the past week, Bianca was glad she'd managed to stay busy spending time with Aunt Winnie, Miranda and Juliet. Making small talk and visiting with her grandfather some helped to keep her mind off her nagging fears. Whatever she found probably wouldn't bring her any joy. But closure might help, at least. Which was why she was so eager to hear what the investigator had found.

She'd also done some research on her own, careful to keep things quiet. Leo was her only confidant in all of this, even though she'd only been able to talk to him on the phone since their one lunch together.

And thank goodness I had him, she thought now. Talking to Leo each night had kept her sane and focused. He was so good at reassuring her, offering her advice, listening. His shrewd business tactics often came into play when he was advising her. Bianca didn't like the way she'd eased into leaning on Leo so much, but it sure did help to have him nearby. He was neutral on all of this, an objective outsider who could see things from a different, less emotional angle.

Explaining to Miranda and Aunt Winnie that she planned to stay in Stoneley at least two weeks, Bianca managed, under the ruse of working on her upcoming case, to close herself up in the vast library across from her father's study in the back of the first floor, but only when she was sure her father wouldn't be home. There she'd pored over family documents and old photo albums, taking copious notes just as she did when preparing for a real case. Except this case was personal and had nothing to do with corporate law.

This was all about family law. Or, more specifically, about how one family could create its own law, without benefit of government or police or any type of authority except Blanchard policies and procedures. But even after her careful documentation, about the only thing Bianca had was a colorful history of Blanchard Fabrics and a family tree that included the grandmother named Ethel who'd died before any of the sisters had been born. Howard never remarried after Ethel's death. There hadn't been very much mentioned about her mother.

But she wasn't about to stop there. Glad that she'd told Juliet what she was doing, Bianca remembered their conversation from a few days before.

"I think there is a good possibility that Mother might be alive," she'd told Juliet when they were finally alone in Bianca's room on the night they'd all shared one last dinner together before the others had to travel back to their own homes. She'd hated blurting it out that way, but what choice did she have?

"What do you mean?" Juliet had asked, sinking down on Bianca's bed to stare at her. "What are you saying?"

"I'm saying that the date on this picture has put all sorts of doubt in my head, Juliet. And I wanted you to know what I'm doing."

Juliet turned pale and silent. "What *are* you doing?"

"I hired a private investigator—just to give me the facts, starting from the night Mother died. I've asked him to trace Mother's relatives and to find out whatever he can about anything that might seem suspicious about her death. And…I'm going to do some research myself, here in our library, to see if anything connects."

Juliet had held her arms tightly against her

stomach, rocking on the bed. "You're really scaring me, Bianca. You don't think—"

"Do I think our father might be hiding the truth from us? Yes, I'm beginning to think that." Then she'd touched a hand to Juliet's arm. "I've felt it each time I've come home. Something isn't right. No one talks about Mother. No one wants to admit that her death was…just brushed aside. After seeing that photograph, I have to find out the truth. And I'm sorry if that upsets you, but I wanted you to know. I haven't told anyone else, except Leo."

Juliet shot off the bed. "Leo? Bianca, he works for our father! He'll probably go right to him and tell him everything. And you know what will happen then."

"Leo isn't going to do that."

"And how do you know he won't?"

Bianca couldn't explain that certainty. "I just do. He promised to help me. He's worried that I'll get hurt or run into trouble. We can trust him, Juliet."

"What about Miranda and Aunt Winnie?"

"I don't want to involve them right now. They're both very loyal to Daddy. The less they know the better, for their own sakes. We'll tell them if we find out something different."

"Different? As in, if we find out our mother might be alive?" Juliet had paced at the foot of the four-poster bed, the light from the nearby fringed lamp casting her face in golden shadows. "I can't even wrap my brain around this—Mother, *alive?* But if she is, why wouldn't she contact us? Why would she stay away?"

"Think about it," Bianca had said, coming to stand by her. "What if she can't get in touch with us? What if she's in hiding, or worse, being held somewhere against her will?"

Juliet had moved her head back and forth, the denial clear in her eyes. "Bianca, honestly, this is sounding a little far-fetched, don't you think?"

Bianca wondered that same thing herself. "I've thought about nothing else since I saw that picture. The date has to be a clue—maybe Mrs. Santiago and Mother were sending us a message, in case someone found the picture one day."

"That's crazy."

"Not as crazy as the way our own father acts sometimes. He gets furious whenever we mention Mother. Aunt Winnie pretties things up for us, but I think she either knows or suspects something, too. And Grandfather, well, he practically threw you down the stairs because he thought you were Mother. When you put all that together with the picture and the date, it—"

"It makes things look very suspicious," Juliet finished, her eyes going wide. "Bianca, this could be dangerous."

"I'll be okay. Leo will help me and I'm being very careful. I just want you to keep your eyes and ears open for me, while we're both here together."

"But I'm leaving in two days. Will you be all right?"

Seeing the newfound worry in Juliet's eyes, Bianca had reassured her sister she'd be safe. "I promise. I'll call you if I hear anything at all, either way." Then she'd hugged Juliet close. "Don't get your hopes up. I'm probably imagining things, but…what if I'm not?"

What if I'm not? She thought about what she'd read late last night, in Aunt Winnie's library, chills moving up and down her spine. "'To sleep, perchance to dream.'"

That quote had come from Hamlet, and he had been thinking of suicide when he'd said it. A horrible deed had just about driven Hamlet mad, so he went on to seek revenge against that deed, and in his anguish, he'd realized sleep might not bring him the peace he needed.

So what did that mean? What had her mother been trying to tell Bianca? To live, to seek answers, to find some sort of peace in dreams here on earth, instead of escaping to death? Or did it mean Trudy herself had planned to seek revenge in some way by staying alive, her dreams shattered but her goal clear? The worst—it could have been her mother's way of telling Bianca she couldn't take living anymore, so she wanted "to die, to sleep no more." Bianca had read and reread the passage, but could find no answers in Shakespeare's eloquent words.

So she'd just have to rely on her own devices, including her very human source.

Bianca glanced up as a late-model dirty blue car whirled into the parking lot. Garrett McGraw swaggered into the coffeehouse, a folder in his hand.

"Mr. McGraw."

He slipped into the chair across from her. "Hello, Ms. Blanchard. Good to see you again."

Bianca itched to grab the folder, but she managed to wait for him to order a cup of coffee and a piece of apple pie.

"What do you have for me?" she asked after the waitress left.

The investigator dug into the fresh pie, swallowing a couple of bites before he answered. "Well, that depends. I've found out plenty of interesting tidbits, but none of them add up."

"Tell me," she said, her whole body as tense and high-strung as the riggings of a sailboat. "I have to know."

He leaned close, his tiny eyes leering toward her. "Let's start at the beginning. First of all, we know the accident was questionable to begin with. Stormy night, slick roads. The whole going-over-the-cliff scenario."

Bianca drew in a sharp breath, then blocked the images his description invoked. "Just get to it, Mr. McGraw."

"I'm getting there," he said, holding up a hand.

"Okay, here's the deal. Your mother's car was destroyed. Or that's the word I get from what few records I could find. No photos, no newspaper reports, nothing about what happened that night, anywhere in this town. That's odd enough. But the car seemed to have disappeared. I've talked to two different wrecker companies and they checked the records—they don't have a thing about picking up your mother's car that night."

"It's been a long time," Bianca said, her mind spinning. "Maybe the records are stored somewhere else."

"I don't think so. Both companies had backlogs for years, some on paper and some computerized."

"Were you discreet?" Bianca asked, fearing her father would hear of this.

"I told them I was doing some research on accidents on Ocean Drive, for an insurance company. They bought it."

She breathed again. "What else?"

"You said your mother was cremated, right?"

"Yes, that's right. Her ashes are entombed in the family vault."

"Well, then, she must have been cremated in another town. The funeral home here doesn't have any verification of that. The funeral director is dead, but I had a nice chat with his son. I told him I was doing a study on cremation verses the regular style of being buried, you know. I found cremation records from way back, but not one on Trudy Blanchard. Not a one."

"But…we saw the urn."

He finished off his pie, then drained his coffee. "Did you see what was in the urn?"

Bianca shook her head, feeling sick to her stomach. "No, we were children. Why would we question that?"

"Exactly. Why would you question anything, right? And with your grandfather and father being so all-fired powerful, who else would question them? There's no autopsy report, no report from the mortician, who would have probably served as the coroner back then, and I even called the old man's widow, on the pretense of writing a book about mysteries in Maine. She was a bit scatterbrained, but she said she remembered her husband commenting on this particular accident."

Bianca held a hand to the scarf at her throat. "What did she say?"

"That your father had insisted on hiring some fellow in Portland to do the work. She said her husband was mighty affronted that he never even saw the body. She never forgot that, that's for sure. Gave me an earful about how your father was so upset and that he wanted to keep things quiet. Rumor was it was suicide."

"Suicide?" Bianca gasped, grabbed at her cup of coffee, her mother's cryptic quote sounding throughout her mind. "You mean, no one here ever saw my mother's body?"

"That's the way it looks, yes, ma'am." He lowered his head, glanced around. "And I can't find any record of her cremation in Portland, either."

"What about the police? They would have had to work the accident, right?"

He tapped a finger on the table. "Remember, I couldn't find any *official* report. And I didn't dare snoop too much down at the station. Chief Marcell already hates my guts. And that assistant of his isn't very forthcoming, either. That would have sent up red flags right back to your father."

Bianca couldn't argue his logic. "And let me guess—there were no witnesses, right?"

"You got it. None that I could find, anyway."

Bianca's mind whirled like the artsy rooster weathervane near the coffeehouse sign outside. A questionable accident. No police report. No medical report. No car. No body. And a quick cremation. With nothing regarding this terrible tragedy ever mentioned or discussed since.

And now, a photo dated after her mother's death.

"It's all a cover-up," she whispered, not even realizing until the investigator nodded that she'd spoken out loud.

"I have more," he said, fingering his goatee.

Bianca could feel tiny beads of sweat popping up along her forehead. "What?"

"First, I'm still working on tracking down relatives. Your mother must have burned all her bridges there."

"No," Bianca replied. "She was close to her parents, even though they didn't see each other after she met Father. I know that from Aunt Winnie. Keep searching on that angle."

"Okay. I'll do some more checking. Meanwhile, I think I've found you a solid lead, but in another direction altogether."

"What do you mean?"

"I went through some records down at the courthouse, just to see if there had been any dubious property transfers, things like that. You'd be surprised what you can piece together, you know, connecting a name to various other things. If your mother is in hiding, there might be something, somewhere. A payoff here or there—"

Bianca felt a headache coming on. "Just tell me what you found, Mr. McGraw."

"I found a Chicago phone number, on some rental documents. Looks like somebody in your family might have connections there." He handed her the folder. "And there's an address in there, too. But it doesn't match with the phone number. The address is for some sort of strange hospital or medical facility—Westside Medical Retreat. I'll leave calling that number up to you. Maybe whoever answers can explain things for you."

"How do you know the two are connected?"

He leaned so close Bianca could smell his cheap aftershave. "Honey, you don't want to know how I found that address, but let's just say your old man keeps meticulous records and, lucky for you, I know how to hack into things like that."

Bianca's hair stood up on end. "You hacked into my father's accounts and personal records?"

"Not all of them. Just the ones that were kinda out there on the fringes, hidden under corporate names. Of course, property information is mostly public record. Then I matched this to that and came up with some interesting stuff. Man owns a lot of property, all over New England, maybe as far as New York. I got to wondering, now who would be living in this property in Chicago? Then I thought about all the other aspects of this case."

"What's this got to do with my father?" Bianca asked, afraid she already knew the answer.

Garrett leaned back in his chair, his smile smug and sure. "I've always been of a mind, when a spouse dies suddenly or disappears mysteriously, check with the surviving spouse first." He held his fingers up like a gun, then popped his mouth shut as he mocked shooting that gun. "Bingo."

Bianca grabbed the file, then said, "How much do I owe you?"

"It's in there. I invoiced my hours."

"Thank you," she replied, shaking all over. "I'll let you know if I need your services again, Mr. McGraw."

"Do you want me to keep looking for relatives?"

"Yes."

"I'll be in touch." He got up, threw some bills on the table, then left.

Bianca sat staring at the manila file in her hands, her mind reeling. Could it be true? Had her own father staged her mother's death? Or had Trudy done that herself? But why? Why would either of them go to such extremes?

Your mother loved all of you.

She heard Aunt Winnie's voice echoing through her throbbing pulse. Aunt Winnie was always trying to reassure them. But was she also trying to protect them from their own parents?

Then she heard her mother's haunting words.

"'To sleep, perchance to dream.'"

Had her mother chosen a chance to dream over the love of her family? Or had that been her final farewell before she tried to kill herself? Had Trudy left their father, so desperate to get away from him that she was willing to give up her children, too? Ronald had told them Trudy had planned to abandon them, but what if she never made it? What if someone had stopped her? Or what if it was true? What if her mother had tried to leave, or tried to take her own life? She could have survived, only to be put away, too dangerous to be around her children.

Had Ronald lied to them to spare them the pain of Trudy's mental state and what he considered her abandonment?

Bianca couldn't believe that. But something had caused her mother to leave the house that night. And like the detective who'd just filled her in, Bianca was leaning toward that someone being her own father, Ronald Blanchard.

Leo checked his watch. Too late to call Bianca for lunch. Maybe he could persuade her to go to dinner with him tonight instead. They hadn't seen each other since their lunch together days ago, but they'd talked on the phone several times. And Leo really wanted to know what Garrett McGraw had found out regarding Trudy Blanchard's accident.

You promised you'd help her out, he reminded himself.

"But she asked you to give her some time," he said, wishing he hadn't promised her that, too. When they'd talked on the phone two days earlier, Bianca had explained that she planned to spend most of her time doing a little recon work on her own. Apparently, the woman liked her space.

Leo couldn't blame her. He had come on a bit strong at first. But his motivation had been completely different then. He'd had a mission to accomplish. Funny how one beautiful smile and a shy glance could change a man's whole perspective.

Funny how he'd been avoiding Ronald Blanchard by busying himself with work.

If he had to report to Ronald regarding how things were going with Bianca, he would have to be honest.

Yes, sir, I've got her interested.

No, sir, she doesn't have a clue what I'm up to.

Yes, sir, I think I'm making progress.

No, sir, she won't suspect a thing.

All of that would be true. But if Leo went back and thought about each of those answers, he'd know that he wouldn't be able to tell his boss the real ambition behind his quest to win over Bianca.

She was interested. But so was he, because she was so very *interesting.*

She didn't have a clue that Leo was interested back. Well, maybe a little bit of a clue, based on how he seemed to call her every day.

He was making progress, but Bianca was shy and used to doing things her way. She didn't quite trust him—maybe with investigating her family, but not with her heart.

And no, she wouldn't suspect that he truly cared about her well-being. Truly. Not just as a friend, or as a favor. He wanted to help her and protect her.

But mostly, he just wanted to see her smile again and again. So he took a deep breath, picked up the phone and waited for her to answer her cell.

She did, on the second ring. "Leo, I'm so glad you called." She sounded breathless.

Leo grinned. "Well, that's the kind of greeting I like from a woman."

Then he heard the fear in her next words. "I think I'm being followed. There's a car…"

Her voice faded out, while Leo's heart stopped beating and dropped to his feet. "Bianca? Bianca, are you there?"

The phone went dead. Leo sat there staring at it, his whole body shocked into a stunned silence. Then he frantically started punching Bianca's number, praying he'd hear her voice again.

SEVEN

Bianca pulled off onto a lookout point on Ocean Drive, her heart beating against the wool of her beige coat.

"Okay, that was weird."

She dialed Leo's number again, her hands shaking. She needed to hear his voice. "Leo?"

"Bianca, are you all right?"

He sounded as scared as she felt right now. "I'm fine. My service faded out just as I was rounding the curve—" She stopped and gasped. "Just as I was rounding the curve where my mother supposedly died."

"And the other car? You said you thought someone was following you?"

"I'm not sure. It seemed like it. I think I saw that same car the other day, when I first met with Garrett McGraw. Then today, well, the car just got so close."

"But you're okay now?"

"Yes. The car was right on my bumper, then it sped away."

"Where are you?"

"I'm still on Ocean Drive. The lookout point."

"Stay there. I'm coming to get you."

"No, don't do that. I…I want to see you. But let's meet somewhere else."

"Are you sure?"

"Yes, meet me at Blanchard Manor. My father won't be home for dinner, and Aunt Winnie will be out for the evening. We can have some privacy there."

After assuring Leo she was all right, Bianca hung up. But she was still shaking. Her hands trembled so hard she couldn't turn the key in the ignition.

Relaxing back against the seat, she said, "You're okay. You're just being paranoid."

Never mind that the black sedan had come up so near to her she truly thought her car might be pushed off the side of the cliff. She'd watched the other car all the way from the diner where she'd met the investigator, sure she was being followed. She'd been so relieved when Leo called just as she'd come up on the big curve in the road, only to look into her rearview mirror and find the other automobile right on her bumper. Then her phone had gone dead.

Somehow, Bianca had managed to shift gears and accelerate around the dangerous curve, then pull over. The other car had also sped up, passing Bianca in a whirl of shiny black. And she still didn't have a clue as to who was driving. Just a vague image of a dark hat and glasses. She couldn't even be sure if the driver was male or female.

But she felt sure about one thing at least. Someone in this town had been watching her every move.

Leo followed Bianca into a small, feminine sitting room on the second floor of the house, on full alert as he visually checked her from head to toe. His pulse was still pounding. He could feel it throbbing against his temple. But he ignored that, instead taking in Bianca's pale features and wide-eyed expression.

When she turned to shut the door, he pulled her close, reexamining her with an in-your-face scrutiny. "Are you sure—"

"I'm fine," she said, a shy smile pushing at her frown. She held her arms on his, to keep him from pulling her any closer. "Let's sit down, please. I'm exhausted." She indicated two plush floral chairs angled toward the dainty white marble fireplace. "I've asked for dinner to be brought up here. Hope you're in the mood for vegetable soup and corn muffins."

"I don't care," Leo said, sinking down across from her. "Just tell me everything, and start from the beginning."

"Okay." She pushed at her smooth chignon and let out a long sigh. "I'm even more convinced than ever that my mother is alive, Leo."

"Whoa. You must have gotten a ton of information from McGraw."

"Not that much, but enough to make me think I've got to keep looking." She quickly filled him in on her conversation with the private eye, then handed Leo the folder she'd picked up from a nearby table. "It's all in there." Then she looked down at her clasped hands. "I want to call that number, but I'm so afraid." She nervously smoothed her hair again. "I even took a bath and changed clothes, fixed my hair. As if that might give me more courage."

Leo looked her over. She did look as if she'd gotten dressed for a special occasion. Her hair was lovely, if not severe, and her dark turtleneck sweater and gray slacks spoke of tasteful grooming and understated class. But she also looked calm, too calm. How was she holding all of this together? he wondered. He'd be screaming to the rafters if someone had told him his mother might still be alive. Maybe if he just kept her talking…

Getting back to the immediate concern, he asked, "And what about the car that followed you?"

"I'm puzzled about that, and just a bit afraid. Not so much afraid of the person, but I think someone is definitely watching me. Someone who doesn't want me to find out the truth. I'm almost sure of that now, but it seems as if this person is just trying to scare me." She shook her head. "I was on the curve,

Leo. They could have easily sent me over the edge, but somehow I managed to get to the lookout point just in time. That doesn't make sense, except to explain that whoever it is, is either curious and just watching, or waiting for the right moment. I think I've seen that same car a couple of times before."

"Where?"

"Once when we were leaving the Lighthouse—"

"I remember that," he said, the image of a dark car whirling out of the parking lot right behind Bianca's little Miata sending him a grim reminder. "I saw a car hurrying after you, but I just thought the driver was in a rush."

"Apparently, in a rush to follow me."

"And you think this is the same car you saw today?"

She nodded. "Pretty sure. And…the same type car came barreling around the corner at Garrett McGraw's office, too."

"Any idea who might be driving?"

"No. The person is always wearing a dark hat and glasses. Very film noir, huh?"

"No, more like very real and way too close for comfort." Leo threw down the file, then came out of his chair. Bending in front of her, he took her hands. "You're as cold as ice." He rubbed his hands over hers, trying to warm them. "Do you want another sweater?"

"No, I want the truth," she said, looking up at him with dark, sorrow-drenched eyes. "But…I'm so scared to make that call." Then she let out a shaky laugh. "A first for me."

"I'll be right here," he assured her. Unable to stop himself, he reached up to touch her hair. "You look tired."

"It's been a long day."

Leo pulled her from the chair, then guided her over to a love seat so they could sit together. "Are you sure we're alone here?"

"Aunt Winnie is out visiting a friend. And Miranda knows to give us some privacy. She forced Peg to take a night off, so she's up with Grandfather. My father is at some social function with Alannah. And the rest of my sisters have all gone back to their lives. It's just you and me—and a house full of servants, of course."

Leo pulled her back against the soft cushions of the love seat, wrapping a hand around her shoulder. He could feel the slight trembling deep inside her. "What are you going to do?"

She stared at the fire. "I have to make that call. I don't want to, but I can't sleep tonight, not knowing. I have to find out."

"Then let's do it now, together."

She nodded but hesitated. "I don't know what to do next. I mean, if I do find my mother alive, what then? I can't stay here in Stoneley forever. I have to get back to Boston. But it's so complicated. Everything points to some sort of cover-up. Doesn't it? Or am I just overreacting, imagining things?"

"You have some strong evidence. And you're the lawyer. But in the end, you have to go with your gut."

She pressed her head back on the love seat, her focus on the shimmering brass-and-crystal chandelier. "Well, my gut is telling me I have to make the call. After that, I have no idea. But I intend to figure that out along the way, whether I stay here or get back to Boston."

Leo found the phone, then handed her the folder. He watched as she stared at it, then he took her hand in his. "I'll be right here. We'll figure it out together."

"Thank you," she said, squeezing his hand before she pulled away. Then she took a deep breath and dialed.

Bianca braced herself for what she might hear, her hand gripping the phone so tightly she thought surely the instrument would crack in two. But Leo's reassuring expression gave her courage. So she said a little prayer and willed herself to be strong.

Finally after several rings, she heard a woman's voice. "Hello?"

Bianca gasped, a tinge of familiarity racing through her mind. "Hello? To whom am I speaking, please?"

"Who is this?" the voice asked, sounding raspy and hollow. "What do you want?"

"I...I need to ask you—do you know or have any information regarding a woman named Trudy Blanchard?"

After a gasp from the other side, the line went dead. Turning to face Leo, she shook her head, an ice-cold numbness settling over her. "They hung up. It was a woman, though."

Leo retrieved the phone receiver and placed it on the coffee table, then took her hands back in his. "What did she say?"

"She just asked who was calling. But she sounded so panicked, especially after I mentioned my mother's name. I think that's why she hung up."

"Do you think it *was* your mother?"

Bianca felt a tingle of apprehension down her back. She couldn't stop shivering. "I don't know. I can't be sure." She turned to face Leo. "The voice sounded so similar, but not quite what I remember." Pressing two fingers against each temple, she massaged her head and stared at the fire. "What if it *was* her? I might have just heard my mother's voice."

Saying it out loud, voicing both her greatest hope and her worst fear, only brought Bianca even more shudders and shivers. Her body seemed to turn to jelly as the tremors that had started back at Garrett McGraw's office finally erupted into silent and steady sobs. She looked up at Leo, tears streaming down her face, her silent tears growing more and more harsh. "Leo, what's happening to me?"

"Shh." Leo didn't say anything else. He pulled her into his arms and let her cry on his shoulder.

* * *

An hour must have passed, maybe more. Leo didn't care. He just held Bianca there in front of the fire. Someone knocked on the open door with a food tray, but he sent them away. They didn't need food right now.

While he held Bianca, he asked God to help her. Leo wanted to find the truth as much as Bianca, but he hated seeing her in so much pain. If what she'd discovered was true, then her whole family was in for a big shock.

And right now, Bianca was bearing the brunt of that shock. But he wouldn't let her go through this alone. He thought about a verse from Luke, used in some long-ago sermon. That verse seemed to shout inside his head now. "You will be betrayed even by parents and brothers, relatives and friends; and they will send some of you to your death."

Betrayed. Bianca might find out she was being betrayed by her own father. And by the man holding her in his arms.

But Leo couldn't tell her that now, not tonight, after the day she'd just had. He'd tell her soon. Soon, he promised. But for now, he held her tight, hoping his true feelings would overcome any sense of betrayal he had once entertained.

Finally, Bianca lifted her head to stare up at him with red-rimmed eyes. "Why are you here, Leo?"

The direct question threw him completely off guard. Did she have him figured out already?

Deciding he'd be honest about his feelings for her at least, he said, "I'm here because I care about you. And because you scared ten years off my life with that phone call."

"But why now? Why me?" She sat up, her fingers swiping at her wet eyes. "I've known you for years—"

"But that was different," he said, interrupting her. "That was before."

"Before what?"

He lowered his head, unable to look into her eyes. "Before I decided to get closer to you, before—"

She held up a hand. "What made it different this time?"

He'd been about to blurt it all out. *Before your father convinced me to play a little game with you, to win you over to his side. Before I realized that you're beautiful and smart and worth fighting for.*

Not knowing what else to do to prove to her that he really wanted to be here with her, Leo turned and put his hands on her face. Then he raised her chin to kiss her.

Her lips were as soft as new-fallen snow, as sweet as hot chocolate. He heard her gasp, then he felt the tension seeping out of her body as she slumped against him, returning his kiss with a sigh.

Finally, he lifted his head to stare down at her. "Does that answer your question?"

She let out a breath. "Not completely. But it's a very good start."

He pulled her back into his arms, tucking her close then kissing the top of her head. "Why don't you come to church with me tomorrow?"

He felt her chuckle, but it emerged almost like another sob. "Is that your new pickup line?"

He had to grin. "I guess that did sound funny, coming from me, but I really think I need to be back in church. You know, all this with my mother dying, and now, with you and the chance of your mother being alive, I think we need to lean on God for a change."

She looked up at him. "Think God will allow two lost souls like us to lean on Him?"

"Oh, I think His shoulders are big enough for our troubles, don't you?" He shrugged. "At least, that's what my father always tells me."

She wrapped her fingers through his. "I haven't really thought about God in my life for a long time now, even though Aunt Winnie is always giving me gentle reminders. But it's hard to feel close to God. I mean, He took my mother."

"Or did He?"

That caused her to sit up. "I hadn't thought about that, either."

"You've been blaming God for something that might have been caused by human hands."

"Yes, my own father's hands, possibly."

Leo's shock must have registered on his face. "You really think that?"

"I'm beginning to, yes. All the evidence points that way. He wanted to get rid of my mother for some reason and he had the means and the opportunity to do it. I just need to find the motive."

They sat silent for a minute. The fire crackled, warming the cozy room, but Leo had a cold dread in his heart. What kind of man were they dealing with? But then, he knew from experience just how ruthless Ronald Blanchard could be. "He has the power to hide just about anything," Leo said, the dread moving from his heart to a warning burn deep inside his gut.

As if reading his thoughts, Bianca said, "You seem to know that firsthand."

Leo wanted to tell her exactly how firsthand, but he refrained. If he told Bianca the truth now, Ronald would only twist that truth and hide the real nature of their agreement. He'd make Leo look like the bad guy.

Well, aren't you? Leo's conscience prodded, leaving him feeling sick and suddenly very tired.

"Will you go to church with me?" he asked, needing more than ever to be nearer to God.

And to Bianca.

Because now not only did he want to protect her

from the truth, but he might be forced to protect her from the real danger her father could inflict.

"I guess it couldn't hurt," she finally said. "I can't do anything else until I find more evidence, and I have to wait on Garrett McGraw for that. Maybe going to church will at least give me a little bit of peace and some sense of direction. Aunt Winnie always says God can help us through any situation. I'll meet you there."

"No, I'll pick you up," he said, rather too strongly. At her surprised glance, he added, "That way we can have lunch after church and I'll get to spend even more time with you." He didn't tell her his real reason. He wanted to keep her as close as possible, so she wouldn't be in any more danger.

"You don't give up, do you?"

He saw her shy smile again and breathed a sigh of relief. "Not when I really want something."

She blushed at the implications of that. Needing to reassure her, Leo grinned. "Don't worry. Right now all I want is for you to be safe and sound. And of course, I do enjoy being around you, so it's not so hard to make that happen."

"You're very sweet," Bianca replied, her eyes full of what looked like respect and appreciation. "I never knew that about you."

"I'm not that sweet, but you make it very easy to be nice, that's for sure."

"Okay, then." She got up, smoothing her hair

again in that way a only made him want to tug it free. "I'll see you out. I'm looking forward to going to church with you tomorrow."

"It's a date."

After he hugged her goodbye at the front door, Leo breathed a sigh of relief. He looked forward to seeing her tomorrow, too. And he planned on spending as much time as he could with her, so that no one else could get close enough to hurt her. Not even her own father.

He'd see to that.

EIGHT

"I like our new minister."

Bianca was surprised by Leo's words, since he hadn't mentioned the church service at all during their leisurely lunch. "I do, too," she said, meaning it. The service they'd attended in the old brick Unity Christian Church had brought back both good and bad memories. She had a vague picture of herself with her sisters, sitting on the row together beside Aunt Winnie and Trudy. Trudy had been as devout and faithful as Aunt Winnie. Their faith had been one of the things that had bonded the two together.

Until her mother had died. Then another thought popped into Bianca's mind. What if Aunt Winnie, who'd always been so loyal to her father and her brother, knew something about her mother's disappearance, too?

Not wanting to dwell on that now, she told Leo, "Today's sermon sure reached home with me.

That passage from John 16, about having many trials and sorrows here on earth, made me stop and think."

Leo inclined his head, giving her a direct stare. "Yeah, especially considering I thought of another passage from Luke just last night."

"Similar to the one the pastor quoted today?"

"No, today's was a bit more reassuring." He didn't tell her about the other passage. Instead he paraphrased the focus of today's sermon. "But don't worry, because God sent His son to overcome the world."

"I'll try to remember that," she said, scanning the sea below the sloping knoll just outside the window. Bianca felt as tossed and frantic as the chilly water down there. But being in church this morning had given her some hope, as did being in a nice, quiet restaurant sharing a meal with a handsome man.

Leo had suggested the Coastal Inn, an upscale inn and restaurant on Heron Lane that catered to both locals and tourists alike, since it was located within walking distance of the village.

Bianca was glad he had. The inn was cozy and elegant and, since Leo had requested a corner table by one of the windows, they had some privacy. They'd also had a wonderful meal. Now they were finishing up with coffee. "Isn't that view spectacular?"

Leo glanced out at the ocean. "Not as pretty as the view right in front of my eyes."

She laughed, then shook her head. "Leo, you get

more corny each time we're together. Sometimes, I wonder what you're really up to."

She watched as he drew back in his chair. The look of utter shock on his face was at once both complex and startling. Apparently, she'd hit on a nerve. "Leo? I was just teasing."

He seemed to relax then, as if he'd only just heard her. "I know." He frowned then looked around. When he finally spoke, his voice was low and husky. "It's just that—I want you to understand—"

"You're scaring me," Bianca said, sure he was about to blurt out some deep, dark secret. "Leo, is there something you need to tell me, something I don't know—"

"No," he said, his hands resting on the white linen tablecloth, his focus moving downward. "What I'm trying to say is this, Bianca. I need you to trust me. I mean, I work for your father. I like my job, but I wouldn't ever put that or anything else ahead of you. I want to get to know you better. I want to spend time with you. And I really need you to understand that I'm being honest in telling you that."

Still unsure, she asked, "But?"

"But, nothing. Remember, just remember, that since you've been back in Stoneley, my life has changed for the better. I can't even explain it myself, but…I feel connected to you, maybe because of the picture of our mothers together, maybe because that picture has set so many things into motion, but mostly because...you're you. Does that make sense?"

Bianca managed a slow nod. "I think so. Are you worried that I'll remember your reputation instead of what I've seen about you recently?"

"Yes," he said, his chuckle shaky. "That's it. Don't remember and don't believe anything you've heard or what you might hear. Just keep all the things we've shared in your mind. Keep that kiss last night in your mind. No matter what."

Thinking about the kiss they'd shared did bring her a certain comfort, a confusing comfort, she reasoned. But she'd felt safe and secure in Leo's arms. She'd never depended on a man before, she realized. She'd been on her own all throughout college and law school, not really dating seriously because she'd always put her education and her career first. Now she was beginning to see that because the two most important men in her life had both been so cold and domineering, she had probably purposely stayed away from any close relationships. Even though Grandfather Howard had at first been kind and doting, even he'd held back part of himself. And Bianca had learned to emulate the dueling traits of materialist generosity coupled with emotional coldness, no doubt.

But Leo might change all of that. If she could just figure out what made him tick. And what had him so jumpy.

She watched him now. His chiseled features were taut and hard-edged, as if he'd forced a blankness over his face. Maybe he'd been going through something at work? Then it became crystal clear.

"Has my father said something to you about us seeing so much of each other?"

He looked away again and Bianca knew she'd hit on the truth. "He has, hasn't he? Has he threatened you?"

Leo hit a palm on the table. "I've told you before, I can handle your father. I've been working for him for a long time. I know his moods and I know just how ruthless he can be, but I also know how to smooth things over with him, so don't worry about that. I can take care of myself with Ronald."

Bianca wondered about that. She had no doubt that Leo was a strong, capable man, and obviously very good at his job. But if her father set his mind to it, he could destroy Leo in an instant. The very thought sent chills down her. "Be careful, Leo. I mean it. I would rather never see you again then have something happen—"

He held up a hand. "I told you, I'll be okay. Let's forget about Ronald right now and concentrate on you. What have you decided to do next?"

Bianca's unease refused to go away. Though she didn't press Leo on it, she felt sure Ronald was holding something over Leo's head. She wouldn't be a part of that. So she decided to tell Leo what her next move would be, and since that move would mean her being away from Stoneley, things between Leo and her father should come to a safe standstill. After that, she had no idea what would happen.

"I'm going to the Westside Medical Retreat," she said. "I'm going to see if my mother is there."

"Not without me," Leo shot back, his blue eyes flashing with the same turbulence as the ocean. "I mean it, Bianca."

She shook her head, causing her pearl drop earrings to sway. "I have to do this, Leo. I have to know. And I'm alone in this. I can't tell my sisters and my aunt, not without some sort of proof. I refuse to put them through that kind of agony. I've already upset Juliet, just by opening all of this up. I wish I hadn't even told her. I don't want to hurt them or give them any false hope. So I'm alone in this, but before I go back to Boston for good, I'm going there to that hospital and I'm going to find out the truth."

"You're not alone," Leo said, his tone turning gentle again, his eyes holding her steady, his face devoid of the tautness and the blankness she'd just witnessed. Now all she saw was a hard resolve. His eyes held a stubborn, intimidating glint. "I'm going to help you."

But Bianca refused to involve him. "No, I can't ask you to help. You have to consider the fallout. If we're together in this and it's all true, your career at Blanchard Fabrics will be over."

He let out a frustrated groan, then quickly signed the charge bill for the check. "Let's go somewhere else."

Even more confused, Bianca grabbed her coat and purse and followed him out the door, but she wasn't going to let him change her stance on this. She'd made up her mind.

Leo tugged her down the path behind the inn, to an intricately carved white wooden gazebo that sat atop a jutting snow-covered knoll. In spite of the weak sunshine, it was bitterly cold and lightly snowing now and then. Bianca turned to face him, pulling the collar of her heavy wool coat up around her face. "Leo—"

He pulled her into his arms, then took her breath away as he kissed her, the solid warmth of his lips hers counteracting against the frigid temperature. Then he stood back but kept her close. "I have an idea."

"Obviously," she said, still reeling. "You think you can kiss me and I'll just forget all about this?"

"I might be tempted to try that," he said, touching his nose gently against hers. "And I do intend to kiss you, a lot. But will you just listen to me right now?"

Stunned, she could only nod. "Okay."

"Okay. I have to go to Peoria, Illinois, next week."

"I'm sorry."

He gave her a tight smile. "It's not so bad. I have this baby dedication. You know, the family thing—it's important that I be there. I want you to go with me."

She smiled at the image of the consummate career man, Leo Santiago, at a baby dedication. "You mean, like a christening?"

"Yes, and I promised to be there. It's for my six-month-old niece. My *only* sister's baby. She's a real cutie, and I've got the pictures to prove it. Emily Marie."

Watching the way his eyes lit up, Bianca felt a warm glow burning away at the chill. "That is so sweet."

"I told you I can be sweet. But in this case, I do have an ulterior motive."

Her heart hit against her chest. "And what's that?"

"You can come with me. Then while we're near Chicago, we can check out this mental hospital together. We can either rent a car and drive back up to Chicago, or hop a flight. Either way, I'll get you there."

His words settled over her with a slow, snow-flakelike descent. She gasped, a hand coming to her mouth. "You'd do that for me, veer away from Peoria to Chicago to help me?"

"Of course. That's what I've been trying to explain to you."

"But what about my father? What about work? What about people noticing we're gone together?"

"We'll meet somewhere else—at the airport in Boston, or even in Peoria. We'll be in and out before anyone can put two and two together."

"Sounds as if you've done this kind of thing before."

He bobbed his head and sent her a devious grin. "I might be sweet, but I can also be sneaky when I have to."

She leaned her head against his overcoat, her heart caving even while common sense told her this wasn't wise. "I still don't think you should get involved."

He lifted her head. "Bianca, I *am* involved. I'm involved with you. Let me help you."

Bianca didn't have time to respond. He kissed her again, causing any lingering doubts she might have had to vanish in a cold, swirling mist. That mist was replaced by Leo's warmth and strength. And suddenly Bianca realized maybe God had heard some of her unspoken prayers after all.

He'd sent her a hero. So why was she denying that?

She decided she no longer would. She returned Leo's kiss with a newfound joy and a trembling hope. Then she pulled back and nodded. "Okay, I need your help, Leo. We'll do this together. But we're going to be very careful."

"I can do careful."

"Good." She touched a finger to his hair. "I need you to promise me that."

"I promise. And I need you to do the same. You're risking everything, Bianca. Not just with this hunch, but by being with me. We're in this together from here on out, no matter what." Then he whispered close, "Say it. Say, 'No matter what.'"

"No matter what," she said, the simple pledge sealing them together. And because it seemed so binding, so sure and solid, she said it again, "No matter what."

He grabbed her hand, kissed her cold fingers, and as they stood there in the white gazebo, with winter snow all around them and the ocean crashing below them, Bianca realized something else about Leo.

In spite of the cold shell she'd erected around her emotions, Leo Santiago had somehow managed to melt her heart.

The next morning at work, Leo found a note on his desk to see Ronald. Dreading the meeting, he marched down the hall to the big corner office where Ronald spent most of his time. He found Ronald standing at the wide long window, staring out at the trees and bluff and the bit of ocean beyond.

"Ronald?"

Ronald turned on his expensive Italian loafers. "Leo, come in." As always, he struck a practiced pose of head honcho and all-around important person.

That pose used to intimidate Leo. But this morning, it didn't. He was no longer in awe of Ronald Blanchard. Because he was now awestruck by the man's daughter instead.

He put on his game face. "You wanted to see me?"

Ronald's condescension was palpable. "Yes. I see you've asked for a couple of days off at the end of the week."

Leo nodded, careful to keep a blank expression on his face. "I have to go to my niece's dedication service, remember?"

"I remember," Ronald replied, rocking back and forth on his heels, his hands tucked into his trouser pockets. "But Leo, this is a crucial time. You're supposed to be reporting in to me, regarding Bianca. I haven't heard any positive news from you. In fact, if I didn't know better, I'd think you've been avoiding me. That doesn't seem right, considering we had a deal."

"I've been seeing her," Leo said, going with honesty. "In fact, we had lunch together yesterday, just after we attended church together."

"So I've heard. Seems the whole village is gossiping about spotting you two together here and there. Charming, but I don't like getting my information secondhand and I need results regarding business, not your personal affairs."

"You'll get results," Leo countered, not yet ready to tell Ronald those results would be very different from what he had hoped for. "Bianca and I are getting closer every day. And believe it or not, we do talk about business a lot."

"Really? So you've got her believing you actually care about her?"

"I'm working on that." Again, an honest statement.

"And have you approached her about coming to work here at Blanchard?"

"I'm working on that, too." Not so honest, but they *had* discussed her career. Even though she'd told Leo her father was always after her to return, she wasn't ready to leave Boston yet. Deciding to continue in the same vein, he added, "Of course, she's leaving later this week, too. Something about an important case. It's rather urgent, I think."

That much was also true. Hoping God would forgive him the transgression of not telling the exact truth, Leo wondered if Ronald would even care about the truth.

Ronald looked displeased, but he kept his cool. "Bianca hadn't mentioned she'd be leaving so soon. But I must admit, I'm surprised she's stayed this long. She rarely comes home and when she does, she doesn't linger here too long. But this time is different. I guess I can at least thank you for that."

Leo didn't want any credit. "She's been visiting with her aunt and Miranda a lot. And she enjoyed seeing Juliet and her other sisters, too." He wanted to ask Ronald why he hadn't spent much time with his daughters, but then it was pretty obvious the man was self-centered and distant, even with the lovely Alannah.

Ronald moved toward his leather executive chair. "I don't need another social update, I need the specifics, Leo. I need a thorough report. So I do believe that means you'd better find a way to get my daughter back to Stoneley, very soon."

"I think she's planning on coming back," Leo said, pleased at the shocked expression on Ronald's face. "Some unfinished business."

Ronald actually looked scared for a minute. "I can't imagine what that would be." Then he turned smug, but Leo could see the rage simmering in his eyes. "Maybe *you're* that unfinished business. Time to drive things home. You know, Leo, if Bianca falls for you, she'll have every reason to stay here. I don't like the way you've handled this, but if it's a means to an end, I suppose I'll have to settle for that. Just get it done."

Leo felt sick to his stomach. He couldn't respond to that. He wouldn't dishonor Bianca with an answer.

But Ronald didn't let up. "So we're still on the same page. You'll continue to pursue this?"

"When I get back, sir," Leo said, turning to go as he checked his watch. He had to get out of here before he did bodily harm to Bianca's father. "I have a meeting with one of our suppliers this morning, and I don't want to be late." He stopped at the big double doors. "I hope I've answered all of your questions."

Ronald stepped forward so fast, the chair spun around. He'd turned from smug to full-blown anger again. Pointing a finger, he said, "If you're hedging,

Leo—I hope you remember our earlier talk, but just in case you don't, let me remind you. I own you. I pay your salary. I orchestrated this plan. You were ordered to do my bidding. If you can't stick to the original plan, then you might want to consider finding work elsewhere, preferably out of the state, since no one will hire you when I get through with you."

Leo should have been scared. Instead, he felt sorry for Ronald Blanchard. He'd used his power and greed so long to get what he wanted, the man didn't even seem real anymore. He didn't want Bianca back because he loved her and wanted to spend time with her. He just wanted to control her, and probably now more than ever since she'd confronted him with that photograph. He'd lost his humanity and compassion. Leo didn't intend to do the same thing.

He held his hands out in frustration. "Ronald, you can't have it both ways. If you want me to get closer to Bianca, then you have to understand we might develop feelings for each other."

"I don't want feelings. This is business. You have a duty to deliver on our agreement. That doesn't include losing your head in the process."

"I know my duty, sir," he said. "I know what has to be done."

Ronald seemed to anger even more in the eye of Leo's calm. "Do you?" he shouted. "Because your duty wasn't to fall in love with my daughter. You're not good enough for any of my girls."

"I never said I was."

"But you're thinking that. I can see it in your eyes. You're letting your heart rule out over your head. I won't stand for that."

But he would stand for hurting "his girls," Leo thought, bile rising in his throat. Was there any good left in this man?

Leo marched a couple of steps back into the room. "You don't know what's in my heart, Ronald. And you really should stop worrying about Bianca. It's going to all turn out the way it was meant to turn out."

"Oh, really? Well, don't be so smug, Santiago. I don't think I can see you in the picture either way."

Leo turned to leave again. "I'm not smug, I can assure you of that. I hate what I'm doing to Bianca."

Ronald's laughter echoed out into the hallway. "You love this, you know you do. You love the power and the position. I *own* you, Leo. Remember *that.*"

Leo ignored the laughter and the declarations. He didn't intend to let Ronald Blanchard win this time. Because there was a new plan in place, and he was the one in control now, with God's help and Bianca's trust. He prayed.

And that plan was to win Bianca over, all right. He wanted her to trust and respect him. He wanted her to love him. Only him. That was his plan now.

No matter what.

NINE

Bianca closed her cell phone, hoping the conversation she'd just had with one of the senior partners back in Boston would suffice until she could get back to work. She'd stretched this vacation to the limits, and the powers-that-be at Burns and Collins were getting a bit antsy since they had a big case coming up in a few weeks. She'd just have to burn the midnight oil once she returned to Boston, but for now she had another case to investigate.

Glancing around the small airport in Peoria, she watched for Leo. They'd been very careful to take separate flights. Bianca hadn't had to give Aunt Winnie and Miranda an explanation. They just assumed she was heading back to work, and she didn't correct them when she'd hugged them both goodbye. Since she'd driven from Boston, it was just a matter of driving south on I-95 and stashing her car at the airport in Portland. Leo had flown out of the regional airport back in Stoneley. They were to meet here at ten in the morning and rent a car to drive to his sister's house.

Smiling as she checked her watch, Bianca remembered Leo telling her that he'd arranged for her to stay with his sister, while he'd be staying with his dad in the garage apartment on his sister's property. He didn't want any hint of impropriety.

So sweet, Bianca thought now. In spite of her nervousness about going to Westside Medical Retreat, she felt at peace and completely safe knowing Leo would be with her. She didn't know what she'd find there, and having him to lean on would help, either way. This leaning-on business wasn't so bad, after all. Bianca found herself relying on God's strength and wisdom more and more these days, right along with her need to turn to Leo. But she didn't plan on getting used to Leo being around. Now, God, that was a different matter. She wondered why she'd waited so long to turn back to her faith, the faith her mother had instilled in Bianca and her sisters from the very beginning.

Oh, Mother, are you out there somewhere, keeping the faith? Are you praying that we find you?

Bianca felt a hand on her arm and turned to find Leo standing there with his overnight bag in one hand and a latte in the other. "Hi," he said, taking a long breath.

"Hi, yourself," she said, letting out her own held breath. "You made it."

"Did you have any doubts?"

Shaking her head, she took the latte. "May I?"

"Sure. I don't mind sharing."

Bianca took a long sip of the creamy liquid. She'd been calm up until the minute she'd looked into Leo's eyes. He certainly could bring out all her emotional insecurities, even while his presence reassured her. What a paradox.

Guiding her toward the car rental counter, he said, "Did you have any trouble getting away?"

"No, but don't make it seem so illicit. I called Juliet to let her know what's going on, but I feel horrible, not telling Aunt Winnie and Miranda the truth."

"You have your reasons. You're protecting them."

"And what about you? How did you smooth this trip over with my father?"

"He knew I'd already planned on taking a few days off to come here. No big deal."

Bianca wondered about that. Ronald had probably made it a very big deal, whether he knew she was involved or not. Her father expected his employees to be at his beck and call all the time.

"Same here," she said, explaining to Leo how she'd handled saying goodbye to her father. She'd gone to his study and stood at the door, bitterness at seeing Alannah sitting on a nearby leather couch causing her to seethe.

"Daddy, I'm leaving now."

Bianca had heard them quarreling earlier, and now Alannah was pouting prettily, one expensively clad foot swinging back and forth.

Ronald had glanced up, surprised at first probably because she had called him Daddy, and second, because she'd even come to tell him goodbye at all.

"You're still angry with me, aren't you?" she asked, hoping he could give her some clarity but afraid to say too much in front of Alannah.

Ronald didn't look her in the eye. Instead, he'd let out a long sigh, sending a cautious glance toward the woman on the sofa. "I just don't think it's wise to…put yourself in such a predicament, Bianca. Or to put this family in such a dangerous position. You need to let the matter rest."

"What matter?" Alannah asked, suddenly perky again.

"Nothing for you to worry about," Ronald replied, his tone brooking no argument.

Alannah had gone back to pouting.

And Ronald had gone back to studying the papers on his desk, forcing Bianca to say, "I'm sorry you feel that way." Then she'd told him, "I'll see you soon."

"So I gather he's still in denial," Leo said now, his eyes full of sympathy.

Bianca nodded. "He didn't seem in the least worried about me or any of this, either. But he sure didn't want me to mention the details in front of his girlfriend."

"And he didn't try to persuade you to stay in Stoneley?"

"No, why would he even bother?"

"I just figured he'd try to make you stay longer."

"I caught him in the middle of some sort of dispute with Alannah. They were giving each other the silent treatment. So it was easy to be vague about my comings and goings." Then she pursed her lips. "He did look angry, but I can't be sure if it was all directed at me, or both Alannah *and* me."

"He *always* looks angry," Leo said. "Sorry, I know he's your father."

"No apologies needed." She took another sip of his latte. "Surely the man didn't expect me to stay in Stoneley indefinitely, did he?"

Leo shrugged, then finished off the latte as they came up to the rental counter. "Who knows? He's hard to read on a good day, but if he was having a fight with Alannah, he probably did forget you the minute you left the room." Then he held up a hand. "Let me rephrase that. He didn't forget you. He just put you in another compartment. That man is so good at compartmentalizing."

"You do know my father very well." But she was curious about Leo's comment. Waiting for him to sign papers and give over his credit card for the car, she asked, "Has he talked to you, Leo, about me coming back to work for him?"

Leo turned from the rental counter, a set of keys in his hands. Bouncing the keys, he looked away. "He's certainly mentioned it. I think that's one of his goals in life."

"But why? He knows I love my job. He knows the partners at Burns and Collins. He has to understand that I don't want to work at Blanchard."

Leo checked his watch. "We need to get going." He hurried her out to the parking lot. "Our car should be right over here." His brooding expression was as gray and blank as the parking lot.

"You don't want to talk about this, do you? Which means my father has been harassing you. We shouldn't be doing this. I should have just gone to Chicago by myself."

Leo remained stoic and quiet until they started up the row of rental cars. Then he shrugged, his brow furrowing in frustration and anger. "Bianca, Ronald doesn't take other people's wishes into consideration. He just demands results. And yes, he does want you to work for Blanchard. He doesn't try to hide that at all."

And he'd probably been drilling that home with Leo on a daily basis. "I guess I have him in a bad spot. He's torn between asking me to come to work for him and hoping I'll go quietly back to Boston and forget all about that picture and my mother."

Leo looked torn, too, at the moment. "Bianca," he began, then he stopped, a hand slicing through the air. "I don't know. I don't know how to..."

"It's okay," she said, afraid she'd gone on and on, putting Leo in a predicament. "You're caught in the middle, I know. And I'm sorry. Let's just forget all about my father and his expectations." She touched a hand to his arm. "Leo, please."

Leo finally looked right into her eyes. "Your father is a very demanding man."

"Well, he can stop demanding. I'm not going to work at Blanchard Fabrics. And I mean that." Then she tugged her shoulder bag against her. "And that's enough of that particular subject."

"Good idea."

She saw the tinge of regret and remorse on his face. Did Leo want her to work at Blanchard, too? Then she had to smile. Maybe he did, but his reasons would be very different from her father's. Or at least she hoped that was the reason for the frown on his handsome face.

"Here it is," he said, pointing toward the dark sedan, obviously relieved to have something else on which to concentrate. "I thought this wouldn't be as conspicuous as the sports car they offered us."

"Smart and practical. I like that in a man."

He shot her a tight grin, lifted the trunk and dropped in their overnight bags. Then he opened the door for her. "It's good to see you smile."

"That might change once we get to Westside."

He leaned over as she sat back in the seat. "Well, for now, let's forget all that, too. My sister's name is Anna and her husband is Jack. Anna and Jack Powell. I've told them all about you. Anna has been after me to settle down for years, and I've got her convinced this might be it." He gave her a little flutter of a kiss, his words husky and low. "You might be it."

Bianca couldn't breathe. Leo had practically declared they might have a chance for a future. "Wow, no pressure."

"None at all. We'll enjoy this time away…from everything…and see where it takes us."

"I think that would be nice."

She watched as he came around the car, a slight smile on his face. But she also noticed a ring of fatigue around his eyes, a slash of white lines around his mouth. How did he put up with her father on a daily basis? And how much would this trip cost him if her father found out the truth?

Leo's sister looked so much like him Bianca couldn't help but notice the resemblance. Anna was tall and willowy, and giddy with a warm happiness that radiated to everyone around her.

"C'mon in," she said, pulling Leo into her arms for a hug. Then she stood back to give Bianca the once-over. "You were right, Leonardo. She's gorgeous."

Leo and Bianca both blushed.

Then a male voice echoed from the stairs. "Oh, man, she must be special, if she makes you look that sheepish."

"That's my brother-in-law, Jack," Leo said, waving a hand toward the man coming down the stairs.

"What a beautiful baby," Bianca said, smiling at the gurgling infant in Jack's arms.

"This is our Emily Marie," Leo explained, his grin making him look young and carefree.

Anna took the baby. "Yes, and our diva here wants her noon bottle." She hurried toward the kitchen. "Go on in the den. Dad's in there."

Jack grinned and hurried after her. "We'll be right back, then you can spoil Emily all you want."

Leo turned Bianca toward the sunny den of the house, where a gray-haired man stood by the fireplace. "Pop, this is Bianca. Bianca, this is my father, Bernard Santiago."

"The very one," Mr. Santiago said, pumping Bianca's hand in his. He had the same strength and self-assurance of his son.

"It's nice to meet you, sir," Bianca said, a bit overwhelmed by the casualness of this family. The Blanchards were so straitlaced and reserved by comparison, she felt as if she'd been missing out on something special.

Bernard guided her to a chair by the fire. "Leo tells me you're a hotshot lawyer in Boston."

Bianca grinned over at Leo. "I'm just a working girl, trying to get by."

"Well, to hear my son tell it, you get by pretty good."

Leo patted his father on the back. "I told you you'd like her, Pop."

Bernard lifted his bushy brows. "That depends. How are you at Scrabble, young lady?"

Bianca put her hands on her hips, laughing. "Is that a challenge?"

"Just might be."

Bianca saw that same challenge mirrored in Leo's warm gaze. "Pops is the Scrabble champion around here—just a warning."

They played a very competitive game for the next hour, each winning a round.

Later at dinner, Bianca relaxed and laughed right along with the entire family. Leo's dad told story after story about Leo's younger years and Anna chimed in with a few of her own.

"Our mother used to hold up her hands in defeat every time Leo would try to sweet-talk his way out of trouble," Anna said. Then she'd stopped, glancing toward her father. "We sure do miss her."

"I know," Bianca replied. "I miss my mother, too, even though she…died when I was nine."

Bernard sent her an understanding look. "I wish I could have been more helpful, about the picture. Since I was mostly working, I didn't always get to go to the beach house in Cape Cod as much as my wife and the kids did, so I can't say I was even there the day the picture was taken. But I can tell you this—your mother and Leo's mother were very close. If your mother needed help, she would have turned to Patricia in a heartbeat."

"Thank you, so much, for telling me that," Bianca said. "And if you do happen to remember anything else, will you please let me know?"

"I certainly will," Bernard said.

The cheerful banter changed to a stark silence for a minute, but Leo brought them all back around with another tale on Anna. Even amongst grief, this family somehow outshone her own, Bianca thought. As the night progressed, she fell in love with Leo's family. And she was pretty sure she was falling in love with him, too.

The next day, as Bianca watched Leo holding little Emily in his arms, she felt a lump in her throat. She had been missing out on something special, and that something was a family of her own. Leo was Emily's godfather. That was a tremendous commitment. And he seemed to be taking it very seriously as he listened to the minister with open-eyed wonder and resolve. It was as if a window had been opened and she was being allowed to peek through it, to a world that she had somehow managed to put out of her mind. A world that she had long denied herself because of unsettled issues from her past.

I can't deny myself all that I long for, she thought now. *How I want that, Lord,* she prayed as she watched Leo and the baby together. *I just want my family happy and whole and healed, no matter what I find in Chicago.*

She continued her silent prayer throughout the beautiful ceremony. And each time Leo glanced out into the pew where she sat, Bianca gained a new strength and a new hope that she might actually see that happen, somehow.

Later, over punch and cake in the small social hall of the church, Leo came to stand by her. "You sure look pretty today."

"Thanks," she said, smoothing the light blue wool suit she'd chosen for the occasion. "Luckily, I always have a proper suit no matter where I travel. Goes with the territory, I suppose."

"You are a very proper lady." He leaned close. "But I like you in jeans and a sweater, too. Maybe holding your own baby. I think you'd make a beautiful mother."

"A mother?" She turned to stare up at him, her heart heavy with so many swirling emotions they burst through her head like the prisms of light coming through the stained-glass windows. "I'd never thought about that, until today."

"I'd never considered myself father material, either," he admitted. "Until today."

Bianca saw the sincerity in his eyes. "You're serious?"

He nodded, took her hand in his. "Holding that little baby, then looking over at you. It just seemed to click. It seemed so right."

Bianca looked down, not knowing how to voice all the thoughts going through her head. "It might not happen with us, Leo. We can't predict—"

"I'm certain," he said, that determined glint in his eyes. "I feel it in my heart."

Bianca wanted to tell him she felt it, too, but she was still so unsure and afraid. "I have to get all these mysteries about my mother resolved. I can't make any promises until this is over."

He gave her a reassuring look. "I understand. By this time tomorrow, we'll know one way or another."

"I don't know if I can do this, Leo," she whispered, her knees turning to mush, her pulse pounding a dangerous rhythm against her temple. "I just don't know."

"Hey, come and sit down." He pulled her to a nearby brocade settee. "Do you want some more punch?"

"No, I'm fine. I guess it's just everything catching up with me." She looked over at him. "Last night with your family and then today, well, for a while there I forgot everything, all the pain, all the sorrow, and all the lies. You do that to me. You make me forget."

"That's my job," he said, touching her hair. "And I take my work very seriously."

"No matter what?" she asked, remembering their promise to each other.

"No matter what."

Somehow, she knew he meant that. Now if she could just get through the next couple of days and find out the truth, she might actually have a chance to find a future with this man.

A future that could bring the promise of a sunny home high on a hill, and a soft, cuddly, sweet-smelling baby being held by strong arms. A promise of the kind of life she'd only imagined in her dreams. The same dreams that always held the echo of her mother's voice, so gentle and sure, deep inside the recesses of Bianca's mind.

TEN

Bianca glanced over at Leo as he turned the car into the long, tree-lined road leading to Westside Medical Retreat. They'd finally located the reclusive hospital on the outskirts of west Chicago, nestled away on a quiet, picturesque hillside. The trees and grounds were covered with snow, making the drive up the long road deceptively beautiful and peaceful.

Bianca had managed to stay calm for most of the two-and-a half hours since they'd left Peoria, but now she could feel tremors of apprehension moving through her body.

"My hands are shaking," she said in a husky whisper. "I don't think I'll be able to do this, Leo."

Leo reached for her. "I'm here. I'll get you through." He gave her a reassuring look. "Besides, we might not find anything here. You have to brace yourself for that possibility, you know."

Bianca managed a quick nod. "I know. Either

way, this is going to be difficult. I've never been a coward before, but right now—"

"Right now, you have every reason to be apprehensive. Your mother might be here somewhere. That's a lot to grasp. And that certainly doesn't make you a coward."

Bianca thought back over the past couple of weeks. She'd returned to Stoneley to celebrate Aunt Winnie's birthday and spend some time with her sisters, but the focus of her trip had suddenly shifted on her very first night home.

All because of an image in a picture. An image that could prove to be fatal for her family.

Terrible thoughts swirled through Bianca's mind. She was accustomed to being analytical, to seeing the big picture. As a lawyer, she'd been trained to do just that—examine all the evidence, then tear that evidence apart to find the truth. Her career as a corporate trial lawyer meant she usually dealt in facts and figures, in contract disputes or business loopholes that needed to be plugged, or in crimes of industrial and white-collar espionage.

That kind of ruthless truth was very different from this one. Her work was very cut-and-dried and all business, but this quest was very personal—and based on a gut feeling and her mother's image staring out at her. She wanted the truth now, but she was afraid to really examine and scrutinize all the aspects of this mystery.

Then the unspoken thoughts whirling inside her head came together to form glaring questions. Ronald knew Leo had given her the photograph, because in her anger, she had told him. What if her father's accusations were right? What if Leo *had* deliberately given her that picture? What if he knew something she didn't know? Was *that* the something he'd been holding back from her? After all, he did work for her father, and he kept reminding her of that.

Bianca felt the breath leave her body. She gasped for air, reaching out a hand toward the dashboard.

"Bianca?" Leo stopped the car as they neared the final gate into the hospital. "Bianca, what's wrong?"

Bianca couldn't look at him. She didn't want him to see the uncertainty in her eyes. "I'm okay. Just having some last-minute doubts and jitters."

He put the car in Park and turned to take both her hands in his, rubbing them as if to bring the circulation back. "Take a deep breath. You're going to be all right. I promise. We'll get through this."

She did look at him then. She searched his face, his eyes, for any sign of deceit. "Why are you here, Leo?"

He looked surprised, then resigned as he studied her face. "You keep asking me that. You still don't trust me, do you?"

"I just…I don't know who I can trust. You gave me the picture that started all of this. You—" She had to avert her eyes again. When she looked back at him, she couldn't hide her doubts. "You started all of this. You sought me out that night. You gave me the picture of our mothers. And we both know you've been just as on edge about this as I have. Is that what you've been trying to tell me? Did my father set this up, or did you do it on your own, to get back at him somehow? You can tell me the truth. I just need to know before I go inside this building."

He dropped his hands, realization changing his concerned expression to an indignant frown. "You think I had something to do with this? Something to gain?"

She thought she saw a trace of guilt clouding his eyes, but maybe it was just shock. Still, she pushed on. "If you know something, anything, that I need to know, you have to tell me now. I mean it, Leo. I'd never forgive you if—"

He grabbed her by the shoulders, forcing her to look at him. "Bianca, do you honestly think I could be that cruel? That callous?" At her stunned silence, he added, "I am not your father. Do you understand me? I'm not like Ronald."

Then he dropped his hands away again, his gaze moving over the ancient brick-and-stone Tudor-style building looming in the distance. "I'm *not* like him," he repeated, this time in a whisper. "He didn't know about the picture, not until after you saw it and showed it to him. And believe me, he wasn't very happy with me for giving it to you."

Bianca watched as a darkness colored his eyes.

She felt horrible, even thinking such a thing. "I'm sorry. I don't know what came over me. I'm just confused and scared, and so tired." She touched a hand to his arm. "Leo, I'm sorry. You've been nothing but kind and helpful and I don't know what I would have done without you. But you have to understand, this isn't easy for me. I've been out on my own for so long, I…I don't know how to deal with anyone else actually being considerate to me. I have to question everything and everyone. Especially someone who I've always considered a player."

"I'm not playing with *you,*" he said, grinding out the words in a low whisper. "You have to believe that. Remember, no matter what?"

Tears pricked at Bianca's eyes. What had she done? Why was she accusing the only friend she had right now? Because she needed to lash out and Leo just happened to be available? "I remember. I do. I won't doubt you again."

"Are you sure?"

She saw the hurt in his eyes. "I'm sure." Then she forced herself to face the moss-covered walls of the dark brick hospital. In spite of the pretty countryside, the place looked desolate and isolated. Bianca closed her eyes, trying to focus on the memories of yesterday and Leo's family. They'd been so close just a few short hours ago. Why did she have to go and ruin that? Maybe because she just didn't know how to handle her feelings.

Then she thought of her beautiful mother, possibly alone and scared, inside this place, and felt utterly selfish for even worrying about things with Leo. "Let's get this over with," she finally said, asking God to help her through this night.

Leo started the car up the hill, then pulled it to a stop in front of the dingy beige stone portico of the old building. Bianca hated the silence that settled over them. It was as if the whole world had turned to a whitewashed, snow-covered blanket of silence. Even the soft-falling snow seemed hushed and full of whispers as it covered the trees and shrubs. But Leo's stony silence was the one she heard the loudest.

Leo came around the car, his expression grim as he opened her door. "Are you ready?"

Bianca looked up at him, wishing she could take back her harsh, accusing words. He glanced toward the building, hurt still evident on his face. She got out, wrapped her white wool muffler around her neck. "It's so cold."

Leo turned to stare down at her then, his eyes going soft, all the anger leaving his face. "Don't be scared, Bianca. Don't worry about anything. I'll take care of you."

His words held both a promise and a plea.

Bianca couldn't speak. No one had ever said that to her before, not even her father. Not knowing how to express her gratitude, she pulled Leo close and held him there, the warmth of his touch giving her the reassurance she needed.

And somewhere in the recesses of her tired mind, she heard that same promise from God. *I'll take care of you.*

That echo gave Bianca the courage to walk up those steps, her prayers as silent and steady as the constantly falling snow.

She didn't trust him, Leo thought with a hard-edged bitterness as they walked up the icy steps to the huge double doors of Westside. And why should she? He'd started out on this quest with one goal—to impress Ronald Blanchard by doing his bidding. Leo had wanted to find favor with his formidable boss, but now he had to wonder why. He'd worked so hard at Blanchard Fabrics, moving from being a part-time factory worker off and on during high school and between semesters at college, to an entry-level executive, then finally becoming second-in-command. And while Ronald had always been difficult and hard to read on the one hand, on the other hand he'd given Leo a chance to prove himself. Leo had constantly managed to impress his boss, so why had doing this seemed so important at the time?

Because maybe, Leo told himself, he'd jumped on this mission not so much to impress Ronald Blanchard, but because deep down inside his heart, he'd always wanted to get to know Bianca better. Had he used both father and daughter to get his own way?

Second-in-command.

I've never really been in charge, Leo thought now as he rang the ornate bell underneath the brass nameplate beside the door. *I'm not the one in control.*

But then, neither was Ronald Blanchard.

Leo could see it so clearly now. God was in control. God was the CEO. Right now, God was putting Leo Santiago to the test. And he didn't want to fail. Tired and confused, Leo let out a relieved breath. If he just concentrated on that one thought, that one hope, he might be able to finally tell Bianca the whole truth. And he might be able to redeem himself in her eyes.

Help me, Lord, he thought as he glanced over at her. She looked straight ahead, her eyes centered on the door before them.

Leo thought back over their time together, acknowledged the patterns falling into place. Yes, he could understand how she'd still have doubts about him. He'd never given her any reason to trust him before, so it must have seemed odd that he'd seek her out now. And with that picture in his pocket. Bianca was a very smart woman. She'd keep on going over and over everything, until she'd finally figure it all out.

Including his own real part in all of this.

But the truth was that he'd had no idea what kind

of maelstrom that picture would set off. Or that getting so close to Bianca Blanchard would stir up a maelstrom in his own heart. And Bianca *had* jumped to the wrong conclusion. He had no information regarding her mother, but he did have a lot to say regarding her father.

He wanted to say something to her right now, but the sound of the doors creaking open didn't allow him that opportunity. *Later,* he thought. *Later, when this is all over and she's secure and safe, I'll tell her everything. Everything.*

Until then, he could only ask God to forgive him for his sin of omission. And he prayed Bianca would one day do the same.

"Dr. Brooks will be right with you."

Bianca waited with Leo. After the gray-haired nurse left them, Bianca said, "She's creepy."

"They all are," he replied, leaning close. "And I think we've talked to every nurse and orderly in this place, beginning with that buzzing intercom in the entryway and on to the reception desk and beyond. Too many locked doors and cryptic replies."

"Well, maybe we'll get somewhere now," Bianca whispered. "I'm not leaving until I find out something about my mother."

She'd just told the last nurse they'd argued with much the same thing. The entire staff at Westside had been tight-lipped and evasive, which only made Bianca think they were indeed hiding something.

Now they were seated in a cold, sterile anteroom of some kind. The nurse who'd answered the door had guided them back here after Bianca, tired of dealing with underlings and noncommunicative workers, had asked to speak to whoever was in charge. That had brought out Mrs. Greeley, the hospital administrator.

Bianca explained over and over again that she needed to find out if a certain patient was housed here. She'd even given them her mother's full name. But everyone insisted they didn't give out patient names, nor did they confirm names mentioned to them. It was an issue of privacy, which Bianca could respect. And it was the law.

But she really needed to find a way around that issue and that law.

"Unless you have written proof of permission from a patient, we can't possibly reveal any of the identities of our residents," the dour-faced administrator in the prim white sweater and black skirt had insisted, her darting brown eyes centering on Bianca with a measured control.

"I'd rather discuss that with a doctor," Bianca had told the woman. "No one here seems to know anything. I want to speak to someone of authority before I leave."

"Very well. I'll get Dr. Brooks. He's been in charge

of Westside for over twenty-five years. But he isn't going to put any of our patients in jeopardy, I can assure you of that."

So here they sat, cold and chilled.

Bianca tried not to think about how run-down and wretched this place looked. She refused to picture her mother in a bed in a corner of some cold, gray room, hovering with unkempt hair and dirty clothes. To even think that would break her heart. Maybe things were better behind the scenes, but somehow she doubted that.

"I hope we're wrong," she told Leo, her hand reaching for his. He'd been quiet, too quiet. While she, usually the quiet one, now found herself wanting to chatter nervously. "I can't imagine my mother living here."

Leo finally looked at her. "Me, neither. If she is alive, why would Ronald hide her away like this?"

"That's the burning question. Does he know? Or did someone else do this?" She looked down at her purse, where she had the picture safely hidden away. "He seemed so shocked when I showed it to him. But he refused to talk about it. And I didn't push him. Maybe because I didn't want him to be involved. I've prayed that's not the case." She looked back at Leo. "Has he said anything more to you, anything indicating that he might know something?"

Leo shook his head. "Your father's only concern is himself. I hate to say that, but it's true. He hasn't mentioned the photo to me since that first time, after he found out I gave it to you. But then, no one at Blanchard Fabrics ever mentions your mother. That's a forbidden subject."

"Just like at home," Bianca said. "That in itself is suspicious to me. Always has been."

After a few more minutes of unbearable silence, Bianca noticed a tall, distinguished-looking man in a white lab coat walking up the stairs toward them. He wore fashionable black eyeglasses and held a clipboard in his hand.

"Dr. Brooks?" she asked as she jumped out of her chair, automatically extending a hand to the man.

"Yes." The doctor took her hand, shaking it as his attention moved from her face to Leo's. "And you are?"

"I'm Leo Santiago," Leo said, a challenge in his blue eyes. "And this is Bianca Blanchard."

Bianca saw the doctor's quick step back. "Who?"

"Bianca," she said, her heart bumping and sputtering. The man obviously recognized the name. "Bianca Blanchard. I'm here to find out information regarding my mother, Gertrude Blanchard more commonly known as Trudy. I have reason to believe she's a patient here."

"Who sent you?" the doctor asked, an unyielding frown on his slack-jawed face. Glaring at her, he repeated the question. "Who, I said?"

Bianca dug in her heels, all of her fear and trepidation gone now. "No one. Let me explain. My mother was supposed to have died almost twenty-three years ago. But recently, I found some information to the contrary. And that information has led me to Westside. Is my mother here, Dr. Brooks?"

"I've never heard of a Trudy Blanchard."

Bianca advanced a step. "That's odd, since my research has brought me here. I can retrace all the steps for you, if you'd like. With the authorities present, of course. Maybe I can even get a search warrant, based on the evidence I have. I know all about patient confidentiality and the privacy laws in place to protect them, but if you're holding my mother here against her will, well, that would be an entirely different matter, wouldn't it?" She was bluffing, of course, but Dr. Brooks didn't have to know that. "Now I'll ask you again. Do you have a patient named Trudy Blanchard?"

The doctor's face turned pale. "I don't have to answer that. You both need to leave immediately."

"You do know something about her, don't you?" Bianca asked, all her instincts kicking in. "You have to tell me the truth."

Dr. Brooks looked nervous. He checked back down the hallway. "I'm not at liberty to discuss our patients."

"Is someone paying you off to stay quiet?" Leo asked. "You need to understand something, Doctor. This woman is a highly successful corporate lawyer. She's probably won more cases than you have case files. You don't want her to come after you, now do you?"

"I don't have to speak to you," the doctor said, turning away. "Nurse, show these two out."

The frowning nurse who'd let them in the door appeared out of an office next to the waiting room. "If you'll just come this way."

When Bianca and Leo didn't move, Mrs. Greeley emerged from her office and stood near Dr. Brooks. "Don't make me call the police," she said, her tiny eyes slitted.

"I'll be back," Bianca said, her voice calm in spite of her quickening pulse. "You can count on that. I'll be back with that search warrant and the police, I promise."

"We can't help you," the doctor told her. "And you'll be wasting your time if you bring in the authorities. I'm sorry your trip was wasted, and I wish I could offer you better news, but...I can't help you."

This time, he said it almost as if he really meant it, with just a trace of regret. With that, he dismissed Mrs. Greeley with a wave of the hand and kept walking.

Bianca watched as Dr. Brooks turned to the right and down another hallway. Then she heard a door slamming.

"You were careful?"

Dr. Brooks nodded, then wiped at the sweat on

his broad forehead. "I didn't give them any information, of course."

"That's good. Very good."

He rubbed his wet palms down the front of his lab coat. "They might be back, though. Bianca Blanchard is very suspicious. She says she has proof. Do you know what that could do to me? That could destroy my career."

"Calm down," the woman cautioned, her voice soft and soothing. "We'll just have to make sure that doesn't happen, won't we?"

The woman wore a heavy cream-colored wool scarf and dark sunglasses. Dr. Brooks remembered the first time he'd seen her. She'd come into his office, dressed in cream and black, and smelling like a garden. He'd fallen for her right then and there, in spite of his wife and kids, in spite of what it might do to his career.

None of that had mattered then and it didn't matter now. Or at least, it shouldn't have. But now, he was getting cold feet. Now, he was wondering what he'd been drawn into all those years ago. This beautiful, ethereal woman had pulled him into her web of deceit, had trapped him with sweet words and overwhelming promises, and he had a sick feeling that he was about to pay for giving in to temptation. Big-time.

As if sensing his mutiny, she touched a gloved hand to his arm. "Jeffrey, have I ever caused you any pain? Haven't we always been discreet? You have nothing to fear. Your secrets are safe."

Somehow, Jeffrey Brooks doubted that, but he couldn't turn away from that gentle, perfumed touch. "I hope you're right." He tried to pull her into his arms, but she backed away to pace. While he longed to see her, really see her, for the first time.

She was beautiful, but she rarely showed her face. He'd seen it in the dark, muted and shadowed, and he'd been intimate with her for many, many years, but this woman always held a part of herself back. The doctor didn't question that. He just took what affection he could find from her, and since he was being paid a huge sum to stay quiet, he planned on keeping things that way. It wouldn't do for the status quo to change now, not when he was so close to retirement and a warm condo down in the Florida Keys. A condo where he had envisioned this woman by his side.

"What should we do now?" he asked, hoping she'd come up with a satisfactory solution.

The woman whirled and paced back and forth, the sound of her expensive boots clicking on the wooden floor in front of his desk. "We find a way to keep Bianca Blanchard quiet," the woman said, her pacing coming to a halt. "We can't let the authorities get involved in this. You know my reasons, you understand my fears. You have to help me, Jeffrey, or you won't get another dime from me—or anything else. Do you understand?"

Then she headed to the door. "We have to take care of sweet Bianca and her determined friend before this situation gets completely out of hand. Let me see what I can do. I'll be in touch. And in the meantime, keep your mouth shut and don't let anyone else in here unless you know who they are."

Dr. Brooks stared at the slamming door. In all his years at Westside, he'd never had anyone ask about Trudy Blanchard, let alone come to visit her. Why now? How had this happened? And how had one of the woman's many daughters found out information that had been hidden for close to twenty-three years?

ELEVEN

Leo waited until the nurse had left them, then guided Bianca toward the doors leading out of the building. He could feel the tremors moving through her body, could tell that the effort of putting one foot in front of the other was almost too much for her. But he also knew her well enough by now to understand that her silence and hesitance wasn't just from fear and denial. No, Bianca's mind was working, spinning, deciphering, moving all the pieces so that the puzzle would fall into place.

She whirled, her eyes widening as she looked up at him. "What if my mother doesn't want to see me? What if she's turned her back on all of us because she thinks we don't care about her?"

Leo could imagine that based on the way Ronald treated people, so he nodded. "If she's ashamed, or afraid, she might have forced the staff to send you away. That would certainly be her right as a patient."

Bianca bobbed her head. "Yes, but if she only

knew how much I want to see her, how much we all need to see her, she'd let me in, right?"

"I'm sure she would, but...we can't force our way behind those closed doors."

Then he watched, fascinated, as Bianca's dark eyes locked on a room behind the reception area. Leo tore his attention away from Bianca to read the sign on the door. "Records." Then he shook his head. "No, Bianca. It's too risky."

"I'm not leaving without some sort of proof, Leo. And if that means I have to get arrested to bring attention to this matter, then so be it."

Leo saw the stubborn set of her chin. Letting out a sigh, he whispered, "Okay, but how do we break into the room?"

It turned out to be easier than he had thought. Bianca made a noise, as if she were in pain. And since she was in such emotional pain, the ploy worked. The same nurse who'd watched them leave came running from behind the reception area.

"What's wrong?" the surprised woman asked as she saw Bianca bent over the desk.

"She's so upset, she's having stomach pains. She's just tired and in shock, I think," Leo said, his own concern very real. "Could she sit down back there?" He nodded toward a sofa behind the desk. "And maybe you could find her some water or hot tea, something to soothe her stomach before we make the long drive home?"

The nurse looked confused, but when Bianca moaned again, she hurried them both to the sofa. "I'll be right back," she said, still looking doubtful.

In her moaning state, Bianca whispered to Leo. "Keys, find the keys."

Leo watched the nurse head around the corner, then went into action. Sure enough, a set of keys lay on the desk beside the reception computer. He found the one marked Records and, with a shaky hand, opened the door with a click. Bianca was up and past him before he could even take a breath.

"You get on the computer," she said, "and I'll check the folders."

Leo didn't have a clue where to look, but the screen provided that information. He scrolled the icons and found Patient Records, then typed in Gertrude Blanchard. When the file came up as Deleted, he turned to Bianca. "Nothing here. Any information is gone. Let's go."

"Wait," she said, as she riffled through the color-coded folders lined up with precision in the medical files along one wall. Then she stopped. "I've got it." Pulling out the folder marked Blanchard, she opened it to reveal only emptiness. "They must have grabbed the files in a hurry, since they left the folder with her name on it. Somebody is running scared."

Leo only gave her a second, then grabbed the folder and put it back in the file cabinet. "Let's go."

After pulling Bianca through the door and pushing her back on the sofa, he dropped the keys on the desktop. "We don't need to wait around for that drink, either."

But before he could tug her up and out of the building, the nurse came around the corner, her green eyes full of concern. "Here's some hot tea."

"Thank you," Bianca said, genuine tears misting her eyes now. "I appreciate this. I loved my mother so much. We all did. I just wish—"

The nurse looked around, then leaned close. "I have something to show you, something I think you will want to see."

That brought Bianca's head up. "Where?"

The nurse put a finger to her lips to silence them. "This way."

Leo wasn't so sure, but Bianca was already following the woman. "Let's go."

Leo caught the nurse by her arm. "Where are you taking us?"

The nurse, whose name tag read Jenny, said, "I'm not sure. It might be nothing, but there's a box of things—"

"My mother's things?" Bianca asked, her focus darting from the nurse to Leo. "We have to check this out, Leo."

He couldn't argue with that, but he still had a bad feeling. "Okay. Uh, Jenny, why are you doing this?"

"I have my reasons," the petite nurse said.

Leo could sense her nervousness. Maybe she wanted to help, but she was certainly taking a big risk in doing so. "All right," he said. "Show us."

She took them down a poorly lit back hallway that looked like a service entrance of some sort. "This leads to the wing where we keep the really ill patients," she said, her voice echoing eerily down the passage. "It's restricted. No one gets in or out without Dr. Brooks' approval."

"But you have a key," Leo noted, while Bianca pushed ahead, her chin up, her eyes wide.

"Is this where my mother is?" Bianca asked. "Is she all right? Can I speak to her?"

"Shh," the nurse said on a hiss. "If Dr. Brooks finds us, you won't ever get to see your mother."

Bianca didn't say anything else as the stoic nurse led them past rooms with padded walls and tiny double-glass windows slit into the heavy steel doors. Finally, she came to the end of the hallway and opened a door. "In here. I hid a box of your mother's belongings underneath her bed. Maybe you'll find something to help you."

"Where is my mother?" Bianca asked, her tone frantic as she searched the darkness.

"I can't tell you that," Jenny replied over her shoulder. "This is the best I can do."

Leo took Bianca's hand, but she pushed past him and into the dark room. A sliver of pale yellow from the outside security lights shot through a high barred window, falling across the dreary, padded white walls of the room.

"I can't believe my mother had to endure this," Bianca said, her voice shaky. "Surely she wasn't so sick that you people had to keep her locked inside this horrible room."

Jenny stood at the door. Thinking she was going to turn on the lights for them, Leo looked back at Bianca and waited for what they might find.

And then the door slammed shut and Nurse Jenny was nowhere to be found.

Letting out a groan of frustration, Leo tried the door. Then he turned to Bianca. "We're locked in."

"The oldest trick in the book and we fell for it," Leo told Bianca as they stood huddled in the middle of the small room. "I guess she was on to us the minute you faked that stomachache. Probably had security cameras on us the whole time, which means they also know we broke into the Records room. I knew this was a bad idea."

"It was worth a try," Bianca said, moving around the room to grope at the walls and reach under the tiny bed in the corner. "But I'm afraid there's no box here with my mother's things, if there ever was."

Leo had had a gut feeling about this so-called box before they'd come into the room, but he didn't tell Bianca that now. She'd been through too much disappointment already, and now she was locked in this awful place. So he tried to look at the positive, if there was anything positive in this situation. "Well, at least our dear nurse seems to know that your mother was here. She didn't deny it."

"Or did they make that part up, too?" Bianca asked, her question muffled by the padded walls. "But then again, she brought us directly to this spot. If I can find something, anything, to connect this room to my mother, then it will be worth the trip."

Leo pulled her away from her continuous search. "Bianca, there's nothing here but the walls and the bed. They set us up and now we're trapped."

"What do you think they plan to do with us, then? Kill us? That would be stupid. Hide us away until they can get my mother out of here? That doesn't make sense, but then nothing about this has so far."

He shrugged. "Well, people will know something went wrong when we don't show up back where we're each supposed to be on Monday morning." Then he pulled out his cell phone. "Hey, I've got a signal. I can at least call the police."

Bianca pushed at the phone. "And tell them what? That we got trapped here because we were illegally snooping in patient files? That'll go over real well."

He mulled that over. If word got back to their families, they'd also have to explain what they were doing here together. "Good point." He thought things over again, wondering how they were going to get out. Then he snapped his fingers. "Hey, if we play our cards right, we might be able to convince the good Dr. Brooks to back us up—you know, in return for us keeping him out of trouble. The man has a lot to lose if we're right about your mother."

"Another good point."

She was still moving around the room, trying to find traces of her mother. Then she stopped, sniffed. Falling onto the bed, she pressed her nose to the pillow.

Thinking she was upset again, Leo rushed to the bed. "What is it?"

"I smell my mother's perfume."

"You're imagining things."

She pushed him away, her voice rising in anger. "No, I'm not. Why does everyone think that? I smell her perfume. I remember it. It's a vague memory, and the scent I'm smelling is very faint, but it's here." She tapped her temple. "I remember, Leo. She wore a distinctive scent—it was a special perfume my father had made just for her in one of the little shops down by the bay. Roses and jasmine, something like that. She used to comment on it. She called it her rosewater scent, but that hint of jasmine made it her own. I smell that now, Leo."

"Are you sure?"

He could see her head bobbing. "Very. My father loved it. He always kept her supplied with it—the perfume, the bubble bath, the lotion. Always."

Leo sat there, his cell phone in one hand, watching as her mind went into full throttle again.

She went still, her hand coming to her mouth. "Always, Leo. Don't you see what that means?"

He started dialing 9-1-1. "I'm afraid not."

She stomped her booted foot in frustration, then rushed over to grab him by the lapels. "It means he's still having it made especially for her. It means he knows she's still alive. This would explain why we're in this mess. Why we're locked up in here."

Leo could tell she'd locked onto something important by the way her expression changed. She'd gone from confused and despondent to calm and calculating.

"Keep talking," he said, to get her to do that very thing. Maybe talking it out would at least keep her calm until he could get them out of here.

She lifted her hands in the air, then dropped them. "He knows about the picture. I confronted him with it. And he knows me. He refused to discuss this with me, but he had to figure I wouldn't let it go. He's probably had me followed—that would explain the dark sedan always on my tail."

Leo caught one of her hands. "But Bianca, that car tried to run you off a cliff. That would mean your own father—"

"Would do anything to keep this a secret," she finished. "Think about what's at stake, what he'd stand to lose. I think my father knows I'm here and he had the staff lock me in, just the way he's had my mother locked up for all these years."

Her theory made Leo's blood run cold. "Even if he knows your mother is alive, you can't honestly think he's behind all of this."

"Oh, yes, I can. We have a paper trail leading straight to him—phone numbers, property we think he owns in Chicago."

"We might need to check that property out, just to be sure."

"How? We're stuck in here. Besides, Garrett McGraw is doing that very thing. I was supposed to get back with him next week."

Leo held up the phone, his fingers ready to hit buttons. "I can still call the authorities, get us out of here. We can explain what we've found, see how it stacks up."

She shook her head. "They'll only think I'm as crazy as my mother. My father will deny everything, to the bitter end. And I just wish I could understand why. Why would he go to such lengths to hide my mother?"

Leo stopped the call. "I agree you might be on to something. But even if your mother is alive and is allowed to wear perfume or lotion in this place, that doesn't necessarily mean your father is the supplier. It might just mean that the staff makes sure she has something special."

She waved a hand in dismissal and resumed her

pacing. "They wouldn't go to that much trouble. I mean, it's been close to twenty-three years. It just makes sense that my father would order the perfume."

"Wouldn't that make the folks at the perfume shop just a tad suspicious?"

She stopped pacing. "Maybe, but then, my father has a new girlfriend every few months. Or he could have it made somewhere else, at another perfumery. That would be easy enough."

"Okay, I can buy that." Leo sat back, thinking about the implications. "So the theory is this—we think your mother is alive and that she was recently here at the lovely Westside Medical Retreat, and we think your father knows she's alive and also knows we've figured things out. Which means the entire staff is involved in a major cover-up. Which means before I call for help, I need to place another call."

"To whom?"

"To here," he said, pointing down at the floor. "I need to call Dr. Brooks and make him understand that if he doesn't let us out of here, we'll spill the beans on everyone involved with your mother's disappearance. Even your father."

"He might not care. But my father sure would."

"Oh, I think the doctor will, too. Even a hint of such a scandal could bring down the authorities on him big-time. Just having someone hovering around could cause him to be in hot water. If we can negotiate with him, instead of bringing in the local police, we won't have to answer any questions regarding why we're here. That could get sticky for everyone involved."

"Are you sure you're not a lawyer?" she asked, her smile muted in the whitewashed darkness.

"No, I just like being around lawyers, but only the really pretty ones." He reached out to tug at her coat. "What do you say? Should we call the doctor?"

"I have the number in my purse," Bianca said, already digging for her tiny address book. She called out the phone number for Westside. "At least this will buy us some time. Hopefully, Garrett McGraw will find out about the other property and maybe I can locate my mother. Somewhere."

Leo dialed, then asked to speak to Dr. Brooks. "Just tell him it's Leo Santiago, and if he knows what's good for him, he'll come and unlock this door. If he's not here in fifteen minutes, I'm calling nine-one-one instead. Oh, and we're in Room number three-twelve."

There was a brief silence, then Leo heard the doctor himself on the phone. "What do you want from me?"

"Right now, a key would be nice."

"I thought I'd let you spend the night with us, since you refused to leave."

"You thought wrong, and you weren't very smart locking us in here with our phones. In spite of the horrible accommodations, the reception is great and all I have to do is call nine-one-one and spill the beans. It's your decision, Dr. Brooks. I'll give you a few minutes to make up your mind." He viewed the time on the cell. "It's half past-seven. You have fifteen minutes and then I'm calling the authorities."

"You'll have to explain to them why you broke into our Records room."

"I'll be glad to, right after you explain to them why the lovely Nurse Jenny deliberately locked us up in here. That might make a juicy story for the local papers, don't you think?"

"I could just tell them you were snooping and accidentally locked yourself in."

Leo let out a sigh. "Yes, you could do that. But then, I'll remind you, Bianca Blanchard is a highly respected lawyer who can argue her case before the authorities with finesse.

"And I happen to work for her father, Ronald Blanchard. I'm sure that name rings a bell with you. In my capacity at Blanchard Fabrics, I've been known to negotiate wage disputes for days, sometimes weeks. I can apply those same skills in this situation and keep things tied up here at Westside for a very long time, Dr. Brooks, you know, in going over and over my side of the issue. I'd talk to the media, spin a tale of woe, make things very uncomfortable for you, for as long as necessary. That kind of negative publicity could cause this place to be closely scrutinized. I also know a thing or two about customer service. It can make or break a business, if you get my drift. Think about it."

There was a long silence, then a sigh. "I'll be down as soon as I can."

"I thought you'd see things my way."

Leo hung up, pulled Bianca close, then said, "It's going to be all right. We'll be out of here soon."

"You are so clever," she said, her tone full of awe.

"And you are so beautiful," he replied.

In spite of the cold, sterile room, a sweet warmth came over Leo. He reached for Bianca, taking her into his arms. "You're shivering."

"Just nerves." She clung to him, snuggling close in his arms. "I'm glad you're here with me."

"Me, too." To keep her steady, he said, "Tell me everything I need to know about you."

"Here, now? I don't think—"

"Why not? It'll pass the time. And at least it'll distract you for a while."

"You know all you need to know," she said, her tone tentative. "I don't want to do this right now. I need to think about where my mother might have gone."

"Bianca, we'll find your mother. Maybe if you relax, you'll remember another detail, like you remembered her perfume."

"Okay, all right, but I'm too keyed up to make small talk."

He turned her in his arms. "But I want to know everything. You know, such as...your favorite dessert?"

She let out an impatient sigh. "Blueberry cobbler."

"Okay, your favorite music?"

"Classical and jazz."

"Hey, I like jazz, too."

"Your favorite season?"

Grudgingly, she said, "That's a tough one. I love spring, but I also like the beginning of fall. That little bit of crispness in the air, the leaves turning. It's always so peaceful and pretty. "

"Me, too."

Then she laughed. "And what about you? What's your favorite food?"

He shook his head. "I'm doing the asking here."

"But I want to know, too. I want to know everything, same as you."

That was like a cold slap in the face. He couldn't tell her everything. But he could tell her father the deal was off. He couldn't do the bidding of a man so callous and cold. He didn't even want to work for Ronald Blanchard anymore. And he wouldn't hide anything from Bianca again.

Right now, however, he decided action would speak louder than words. "This is all you need to know." He put his hands on her face, brought her close and kissed her, knowing he might not get the chance again once he told her the truth.

TWELVE

Alannah leaned over Ronald's desk, her pouting lips pursed as she lifted her carefully arched eyebrows. "What do you mean, we can't go on our trip to Europe until later in the spring?"

Ronald's right hand hit the desk pad with a bang, causing his gold-edged coffee cup to wobble. He'd purposely planned a quiet Sunday afternoon, hoping to get some work done here at the mansion. But Alannah had shown up over an hour ago, her noisy entrance disturbing everyone from the butler to Howard's devoted nurse Peg.

"Alannah, I don't have to explain myself to you. If I say something has come up, then that's all you need to know. We can take that trip anytime." He pinched his nose with his thumb and index finger. "Now, I've got work to do. And I'm sure you've got some charity event to attend, or at the very least, some shopping to do."

"Why should I shop now, when you just postponed the trip you gave me for Christmas, a trip I've been looking forward to for months?"

Glancing at his watch, Ronald got up and came around the desk. He had a very urgent appointment and he didn't want Alannah around to see his visitor. "Alannah, sweetheart, now don't be difficult. I've got a lot of problems to handle without adding you to the mix. Leo has been out of town and unreachable, so I'm having to deal directly with a couple of unhappy clients who received only partial shipments of some very expensive upholstery for their custom-designed office furniture. Then I've got to go over Leo's grand plan to make us more environmentally sound by recycling some of our synthetics."

Not to mention, Leo's waffling around a thorough report on his progress with Bianca—and just what that progress entailed, business or pleasure. Just wait, Ronald thought, gritting his teeth. Leo Santiago was going to get an earful when he did finally show up for work tomorrow. Then of course, there was the other pressing issue, that cryptic phone call Ronald had received early this morning. And he was running out of time.

He smiled down at Alannah, hoping she'd be reasonable. "I tell you, if that Leo wasn't so smart and on top of things, I'd get rid of him—taking off like this and not checking in."

Alannah looked completely bored. Tugging at her tailored wool pantsuit, she said, "I don't care where Leo Santiago is, Ronald. But I'm worried about you. You seem so distracted lately. And working on a Sunday afternoon? Honestly, that's just not like you. Maybe we should go ahead and take this trip now—"

"I said no!"

Alannah stepped back, her hands in the air, palms up. "Okay, all right. I'll quit badgering you for now. Will I at least see you for dinner?"

He nodded as he gently guided her toward the door, hoping none of the ever-curious servants were listening. He'd already had to soothe that snoop Peg Henderson. The woman sure didn't know her place. Always telling people to be quiet and stay away from Howard. Of course, she never said anything critical to Ronald. He always visited his father at least once a day.

"I'll try very hard, I promise. Let's eat at home tonight. A nice quiet dinner, here by the fire, just the two of us."

"You mean that? No Winnie? No Miranda or Bianca hovering nearby?"

"Bianca is back in Boston for a few days, and Miranda is closed up in her room, working on yet another chapbook."

"Your daughters are odd, Ronald."

Ronald sent her a warning look. "Careful, darling. They are still my flesh and blood."

"Don't I know it."

Wanting to get rid of her, Ronald didn't argue. "Alannah, I really need to get some things done."

She tossed her red tresses off her face. "I'm leaving. But I'll be back for that dinner you promised."

"Of course, darling. Meantime, why don't you go down to that nice little perfume shop in the village and buy something that smells divine? I'm pretty sure they stay open on Sunday afternoons for the tourists. Tell them to put it on my tab."

Alannah squealed in delight. "Ronald, how sweet. You've never bought me perfume before."

Ronald thought of Trudy and how she'd always smelled so fresh and fragrant, like a rose garden in full bloom. It hurt to think about her, but her face was always in his mind, in his dreams, especially lately, after seeing that picture Bianca has shoved in his face. He closed his eyes to wash away the memories, then opened them back up to stare over at Alannah. "No, I haven't. Now, get going. Please."

Alannah blew him a kiss then pranced out the door.

Ronald turned back to his thoughts. Why had Leo given Bianca that picture? Hoping his inquisitive daughter had taken him at his word and let the matter drop, he waited for his visitor to show up. Just as the clock struck three, the doorbell rang and he heard the butler greeting someone.

That would be his visitor, and right on time. Now to get this over with, so he could get on with the more important business of running Blanchard

Fabrics, a never-ending job, even on a chilly, snow-covered Sunday afternoon. Looking up toward where his father was housed on the third floor, Ronald wished he didn't feel such resentment for being stuck with all the responsibilities of the family business. But it was up to him now, had been for years, to keep the business running smoothly. He'd tried to get away once, long ago. He and Trudy and the girls had been happy in their own house, but that hadn't worked out. That life had ended the night Trudy had left. *Had died.* Nothing in his life had worked out the way he'd planned.

"Oh, Trudy," he said, "what have I done?"

He shook his head, cleared his thoughts and turned to wait for the man who'd insisted he needed to speak to Ronald right away.

Garrett McGraw whistled as he swaggered into the inner sanctuary of the great Ronald Blanchard himself. "Wow, oh, wow. You know, I've always wondered what this place looked like. Fit for a king, that's what this estate is."

Ronald looked across the room at the man, disdain evident in his every movement and in the tone of his voice. "Who are you and what do you want?"

Garrett chuckled, slumped down in a chair without being invited to do so, enjoying the smell of old leather and old money. He figured he was sitting in the catbird's seat, so he could do as he pleased. Because Ronald Blanchard was about to make him a very rich man. "Like I told you on the phone, Mr. Blanchard, I have some very important information regarding your…*late* wife. Information that you probably don't want leaked to anyone. Interested?"

Ronald stood behind his chair, his face a blank. "That depends. I have the distinct feeling anything you have to say to me is going to cost me. Am I right?"

Garrett let out a hoot. "I always heard you were a very shrewd man. And you are correct, but we can work out the details of that later. Want to hear the whole story?"

Ronald sank onto his chair, pulled it close to the big desk. "I'll give you five minutes."

"Make it ten," Garrett said with a grin. "'Cause this is gonna be good."

Ronald waited until Garrett McGraw was through spewing all the intimate details he'd somehow found out about the Blanchard family, then banged his hand on the desk just as he'd done with Alannah, but this time the whole desk rattled. And Garrett McGraw flinched.

"You can't be serious," Ronald said, each word ground out with a simmering rage. Thanks to Bianca's meddling, his quiet Sunday afternoon had gone from bad to worse.

"I'm very serious, Mr. Blanchard," McGraw

said, no longer flinching. "Your lawyer daughter is on to you, sir. She's had me digging facts where facts really aren't even supposed to be hidden. Latest, as I said, is that cute little town house in Chicago." He held up a callused hand. "And I haven't even checked the property in New York. Now, mind you, I never actually approached the occupants of the house in the Windy City, but I know the deed is in your name, and I did see a woman leaving the house several times. So I'm thinking either you've got another honey stashed away near Lake Michigan, or you've banished your long-lost wife to the Windy City and you don't want her daughters to know she's alive. Either way, I hold all the cards. And I charge by the hour."

He sank back, studying his fingernails. "I'm guessing I could make a little extra on the side, too, what with the tabloid tales and a nice story in the local paper that would probably double my P.I. business. I mean, I've stumbled across a woman who's supposed to have been dead for decades. What a coup!"

"Shut up," Ronald shouted, standing up to lean over the desk, his knuckles pressing against the leather of his calendar pad until they turned a dull yellowish white. "If you think you can bully me into blackmail, Mr. McGraw, you are sorely mistaken. You have no idea, no idea at all, with whom you are dealing. Do you know how powerful the Blanchard name is in this town?"

Garrett rubbed a hand down his goatee. "I sure do. And that's the very reason I came to you first, as a courtesy. You can pay me a nice little lump sum and I'll pretend we never had this conversation, plus I'll tell Bianca I'm off the case for good. Or you can explain all of this to your saintly sister and your children. You know, all about that loony bin near Chicago and the possibility that your wife is alive and well and living there, and you can explain about the little love nest near the hospital—"

"I said *enough,*" Ronald shouted, his pulse beating fast, his chest tightening in a painful grip. "You can't pin anything on me, McGraw. It'll be my word against yours. I'll just dismiss you as a greedy blackmailer and deny everything."

"Oh, I don't doubt that. After all, you've been hiding all of this—somehow—for years. But I guess just the thought that your own daughter is digging into the mess must be pretty upsetting, huh? And if she's as sharp as she seems to be, she's probably stashed copies of everything I've found somewhere safe, just in case. I can always mention that to the tabloids, too, for extra measure. What a tragedy, what an ironic twist of fate. It's like some bizarre mystery movie or something, don't you think?"

Ronald didn't want to think about Bianca and her betrayal right now. He'd deal with that later. And he didn't want to dirty his hands with the likes of Garrett McGraw, either. But he had to shut the man up. So he put on his best game face and said, "I'll have to think about this, Mr. McGraw. Let's say I do decide to pay you off. Just how much money do you expect me to give you?"

Garrett rubbed his hands together. "Oh, I'm not completely greedy. Just enough to get me out of Maine and maybe somewhere down south, where the sun is bright and it's always happy hour." He named a price.

Ronald balked inside, thinking he could spare the quarter-million dollars, but he wasn't going to just give it away to this opportunist. So he kept a calm demeanor, all the while thinking of ways out of this predicament. "I'll see what I can arrange, but it will take me some time to transfer this kind of money. Can we meet somewhere later in the week? Somewhere discreet and out-of-the-way?"

"Of course," McGraw said. "I'm a patient man. I'll give you twenty-four hours. Oh, and bring the money in cash. I don't accept checks." With a grin, he extended his hand.

Ronald ignored the outstretched hand. "How about that old park near the Coastal Inn? Not the ocean-side park, but the one across the road, on the other side. It's heavily wooded and should be deserted this time of year."

McGraw nodded. "Say around eight tomorrow night?"

"I'll be there." Ronald didn't move a muscle.

Then he said, "Oh, and I have one very important stipulation, Mr. McGraw. You will not tell my daughter anything about this conversation. I don't want Bianca to know what I've learned."

"You mean, you aren't going to talk to her about this?"

"No, I certainly am not. There's nothing to talk about. If she finds out you came to me and I paid you off, she'll think I'm guilty."

"Are you?"

"That is none of your concern. You'll get your payoff, and then I expect you to leave Stoneley, for good."

"Or?"

"Or you'll regret it, I promise."

McGraw stood with his hands in his jean pockets, then shrugged. "I'm thinking maybe I'd better up the price just a bit."

"You won't get one more dime from me. We agreed on a price already."

"But that was before you threatened me and made me promise not to tell Bianca anything else."

Ronald wanted to strangle the smug man, but he held his anger in check. He could go to the authorities, but that would bring an onslaught of unwanted attention and publicity. McGraw knew that. But Ronald knew how to get rid of vermin. He upped the price by fifty thousand dollars. "How's that?"

"That is mighty generous of you," McGraw said. "See you tomorrow night, sir."

Ronald watched as Garrett McGraw swaggered up the long central hallway and out the front door. Then he slumped against the doorjamb of his study, his mind whirling and churning. "Bianca, how could you do this to me?" he whispered. Then he caught himself and checked to make sure he was alone.

The house creaked and moaned as the wind whipped against the big bay windows of his office. He turned away from the door and watched as snow drifted down off the eaves above. Somewhere in the house, a door slammed.

Ronald didn't pay much attention. He only heard his wife's pleas on the night she'd left. He only heard Trudy asking him to forgive her. Now, he wished he could have that chance again. Just once again.

Bianca hugged Leo tight at the Chicago airport. They were taking separate flights again. He would return to Stoneley while she would go back to Boston for the night. Then she'd drive to Stoneley tomorrow, after she'd explained to the partners that she had an urgent personal matter to take care of before she would be back at work.

And just when she'd be back at work, she couldn't say. The weekend had brought many revelations, the most important being that apparently her mother was alive somewhere. But where?

"Are you sure you're okay?" Leo asked, concern coloring his eyes as he stared down at her.

"I'm fine," she replied. "I'm exhausted, but too keyed up to sleep. I suppose I'm still numb."

He touched a finger to her hair, pulling it away from her temple. "Dr. Brooks won't say anything. He knows we have him cornered."

"I just wish he'd told us who's behind all of this."

"He's too involved, and he's running scared. He's probably making plans right now to leave the country."

"And, legally, I don't have enough proof to stop him. No records, no solid connections, other than the smell of my mother's perfume and a gut feeling."

"We'll keep at it," Leo said. "Somebody will slip up. Meantime, maybe your P.I. will bring us another good lead."

Bianca leaned against him, savoring the warmth and security of being in his arms. "I keep thinking, what if I'd never seen that picture? I would have never known my mother was alive. Never."

He kissed the top of her head. "That picture brought us together, and maybe for a reason. I hope so."

She saw that hope in his eyes, and once again felt as if he wanted to say more. Leo wasn't exactly an open book. He was more outgoing and charismatic than she could ever be, but he had a quiet side, too. She'd seen that side, and wondered when he'd let her in.

As if sensing her worries, he lifted her chin with a finger. "Hey, are you with me?"

"I'm here," she said. "Just so much to absorb. I have to confront my father. But first, I have to tell Miranda, and maybe Aunt Winnie. This will break their hearts. I don't know how we'll tell the others, but sooner or later, it'll have to be done."

They listened as Leo's flight was called. "I hate to leave you," he said, still holding her close.

"I know." She smiled up at him, gaining strength from having him near. "I'll be back in Stoneley tomorrow night."

"I can't wait that long."

She managed a smile. "You have to."

He nodded, pressed his forehead to hers. "I'll call you first thing Tuesday morning. Better yet, you call me the minute your plane lands."

"Okay."

They kissed briefly, then Bianca glanced at her watch. "I'd better find my gate. My flight leaves in twenty minutes."

"Stay safe," he said, walking backward as he held up a hand to her.

"You, too."

Then he rushed back to her. "You don't think Brooks would do anything stupid, do you? Like send someone after you?"

"I don't think so," she said, meaning it. "He seemed as terrified as we are—the implications of the scandal could ruin a lot of lives."

"I won't let it ruin us," he said, a gentle plea in his words again. "I promise."

She kissed him one more time. "Go, before you miss your plane."

His hand trailed down her arm. "I'll see you soon."

"Soon," she said, watching him walk away. She missed him already.

Then she turned and searched the gate numbers until she found her flight. As she sat waiting for her plane to depart, she wondered how she and Leo would work things out. She had to go back to work in Boston eventually, no matter the outcome with her mother. But she couldn't simply drop this. And she couldn't forget her time with Leo.

All the more reason to tell Miranda and Aunt Winnie about everything she'd found. Someone else in the family would have to take over and figure this thing out, to the bitter end. They couldn't stop until they'd found their mother again.

And until then, Bianca wasn't sure how much of herself she could give to Leo. She sure wanted him in her life—that much she knew, without a doubt. She'd fallen in love with Leo Santiago.

Leo sat in the window seat of his plane, looking out at the lights of the city as the plane ascended into the sky over Chicago. He had to tell Bianca the truth, and he would, but first he had to tell Ronald Blanchard that he no longer wanted any part of this scheme, and that meant he had to quit his job at Blanchard Fabrics.

Tired, Leo closed his eyes as the plane lifted into the air. He'd never liked takeoff. Landing was always better. It meant coming home. He thought about Bianca and a warm feeling settled over him. Being with her felt like coming home.

"Soon," he whispered in the darkened plane. Soon, they would both be home, together. He wasn't sure exactly where they would land when all the dust had settled, but he was sure he wasn't going to let her go without a fight.

Because he'd fallen in love with Bianca Blanchard.

THIRTEEN

Ronald Blanchard stabbed the phone pad with shaky fingers, then listened for the connection at the other end of the line. He hadn't slept all night, but he'd waited until reaching the office before making this call. He didn't want anyone at home to hear this particular conversation.

"Hello?"

He sucked in a deep breath after hearing the female voice, then shouted into the phone, "You'd better get things under control!"

"What do you mean?"

Ronald didn't want to give away everything he knew. Better to keep things quiet. Especially with this one. She was a live wire. "I mean things are getting complicated. Bianca is asking questions."

"I'm aware of that. But it's going to be okay. I have people in place to watch out for such things. I don't think we need to worry about her for now."

Ronald doubted that anything would stop his inquisitive daughter. Bianca wouldn't let up. He gritted his teeth, then spoke clearly and concisely. "You'd better clear up this mess, or you won't get one more dollar from me. I'm tired of paying for your mistakes."

"I told you, I'm working on it. Bianca doesn't have any concrete proof." There was a pause. "But I'm going to make sure she stops snooping, one way or another."

The breath left Ronald's lungs. "Don't threaten my daughter."

"Don't worry. I'll just scare her away, nothing more. She won't be a problem at all. She's just...confused."

"You'd better hope she drops this. I mean it this time. One more indiscretion and I'm done footing your bills."

"I'll be in touch."

The woman broke the connection, causing Ronald to slam down the phone. Then he looked up to find his secretary, Barbara Sanchez, standing there with a shocked look on her face.

"Is everything all right, Mr. Blanchard?"

"Fine, Barbara. Just another angry vendor. Any word from Leo this morning?"

"I think he's in his office. Shall I ring for him?"

Ronald didn't have the stomach to face Leo, not knowing what Bianca might have told him. "No, I'll check with him later."

Barbara stood staring at him, which only make Ronald's nerves even more on edge. "Was there anything else, Barbara?"

"No, sir. I'm just worried about you. Is there anything I can do to help?"

"Shut the door and leave me alone for a while," Ronald said, but his tone was gentle now. It wasn't Barbara's fault his life was suddenly falling apart.

No, the fault lay squarely on his own shoulders, and now, his past sins were finally catching up with him.

Bianca waited in Aunt Winnie's sitting room, her palms damp, her heart pounding. She was weary to the bone, but she knew this had to be done. She had to tell Miranda about her findings. She'd called Leo and let him know she was back, and hearing his voice had given her courage, but she hadn't seen her father yet. She'd need Miranda with her before she confronted Ronald.

The door opened and Aunt Winnie walked in. Surprised to see her instead of Miranda, Bianca got up to hug her aunt close. "How are you?"

"I'm fine, dear. The chef told me you were home and up here, so I ordered us some hot cocoa and some tea cakes for a late-night snack."

Thinking she couldn't bear to tell her aunt everything she'd discovered, Bianca put on a cheerful face. "That sounds lovely. Is Miranda on her way up?"

"I think so. She's had a rough weekend."

"Another panic attack?"

Aunt Winnie settled into her chair by the fire. "Well, yes. But not as severe. Your father has been on edge lately, and I think Miranda can sense such things. They had words last night, after Alannah insisted on having your father all to herself for dinner."

Bianca could only guess her father's irritability probably had something to do with her findings, but Ronald probably couldn't admit that. She also wondered if she should add to Miranda's woes, but she had to talk to someone, and she preferred to seek help from family rather than the authorities, at least until she decided what to do next.

A knock at the door caused her to whirl and open it, thinking she'd find Miranda on the other side. Instead, Peg Henderson stood in the hallway, carrying a tray with three mugs of hot cocoa and some cookies.

"Peg, what are you doing, bringing this?" Bianca asked.

Peg gave her a wide smile. "Everyone in the kitchen was busy, and I just happened to be coming back upstairs, so I offered to bring it in for Sonya. Miranda should be here soon. She was going over some things with the chef."

"That was thoughtful of you," Aunt Winnie said, smiling up at the prim nurse. "How is Father tonight?"

Peg shook her head. "He's about the same. He was asleep when I went down to the kitchen. All things considered, I'd say today has been one of his better days. Which is why I took a break and went in search of some refreshments."

"You work too hard," Aunt Winnie replied. "We can always find someone to relieve you, if you need a few days off."

"Oh, no," Peg said, making sure the tray was straight on the coffee table in front of the fire. She refolded the dainty linen napkins to her satisfaction, then stood and straightened her crisply ironed white uniform. "I don't mind the work, Miss Blanchard. Mr. Howard is such a dear, I hate to leave him alone for too long."

"We won't ever forget your care," Winnie said, patting her fingers on the puffy arms of her chair. "That cocoa smells divine."

Peg turned to Bianca, her expression quizzical. "It's good to see you back so soon."

Bianca managed a smile. "Well, I had some comp time coming, so I decided to spend a few more days here with the family."

Peg lifted her head, then touched a hand to her perfectly styled short curly brown hair. "That's sure to be good news for your father. He seems so devoted to his family."

Bianca wanted to laugh out loud, but she refrained. "Yes, I suppose that's true. Have you seen him tonight?"

Peg shook her head, her smile fading. "No. I'm

not sure where your father is right now. He missed dinner again."

Miranda came in the door, glanced around, then walked over to the fire, her long black skirt swishing around her ankles. "Thanks for bringing the tray, Peg."

"Of course. You ladies have a nice visit." Peg smiled again, then left the room, shutting the door behind her.

Bianca stared after the door. "Does her hair ever move?"

"Now, be nice," Aunt Winnie cautioned. "She's a loyal employee."

"Almost too loyal, if you ask me," Bianca retorted. Then she looked down at the sunflower-embossed tapestry rug. "I guess I should be thankful that she does work so hard. Grandfather is comfortable and clean, at least."

Miranda bobbed her head. "Peg is a perfectionist. She rants if there's one speck of dirt or clutter anywhere near Grandfather. His room is probably more sterile than those at Stoneley Memorial Hospital."

Aunt Winnie chuckled. "It takes one to know one, my dear. You two wrote the book on being tidy and neat. And you are both protective of your grandfather."

Miranda shrugged, sank down on a yellow-and-red floral ottoman. "Not even I'm as compulsive as Peg, Auntie." Then she grinned. "Let's pass the cocoa and chat."

Bianca decided she'd wait until after Aunt Winnie retired to talk to Miranda. Right now, she tried to stay positive for Aunt Winnie's sake. And she reminded herself that Leo was going to call her again later.

Miranda slanted her head toward Bianca. "What's that dreamy expression about?"

Bianca's eyes widened. "Did I look dreamy?"

Aunt Winnie leaned forward. "I think it has something to do with Leo Santiago. Is that why you found an excuse to return here so quickly?"

Thinking that assumption could cover a multitude of excuses, Bianca inclined her head, then held out her hands, fingers splayed toward the welcoming fire. "Maybe. Leo and I have grown close."

Miranda reached out a hand to clasp Bianca's fingers. "I think that's wonderful."

Bianca didn't miss the wistful tone in her sister's words. She wanted Miranda to escape the confines of this old house and really live her life. But her sister was afraid to venture too far away. Maybe if they could find their mother, it would help Miranda heal, too.

"Leo seems like a nice young man," Aunt Winnie said, sipping her cocoa as she stared at the fire. "He comes from good stock. His family lived here until his mother died. Now his father lives near Leo's sister in Illinois, I believe."

Bianca nodded. "Yes, Leo told me all about that." She hated not revealing that she'd just seen Leo's family, but now wasn't the time to explain her recent whereabouts. "His parents were happy for a long time. I think he's glad his father has a grandchild to keep him occupied."

"I guess Leo gets lonely without his family," Miranda said. "You've probably helped with that, Bianca."

"As I said, we've gotten close," Bianca repeated. She wasn't ready to go into detail just yet. Her nerves were frayed, and her skin crawled each time she remembered the ugly truth of what she'd seen in Chicago, but she had to refrain from screaming out her fears and worries. She felt as if she were tap-dancing on a wire, trying to stay one step ahead of her father and everyone he'd probably been paying off all these years. And she had no doubt he was doing exactly that, even if she couldn't prove it yet.

"How do you feel about him?" Aunt Winnie asked, her keen eyes sweeping over Bianca. Bianca had been so lost in thought, her expression must have looked blank. Aunt Winnie chuckled. "Leo, darling. How do you feel about Leo?"

"Oh, I care about him, a great deal," Bianca admitted. "But with me in Boston and Leo here, I'm not so sure where we can go, relationshipwise. And then there's the whole issue of Father." She couldn't say just how much her father's actions would color her decision regarding Leo. So much had to be resolved before she could even delve into her feelings.

"What about Father?" Miranda asked, a frown clouding her features.

Bianca had let that statement slip. She had to be more careful. "Well, Leo works at Blanchard Fabrics. And…I don't think Father is thrilled that Leo and I are spending time together."

"Ronald demands complete loyalty."

Bianca remembered thinking the very same thing her aunt had just said. "Yes, we're all aware of that."

Aunt Winnie set her cocoa down and looked at Bianca. "Listen to me, my dear. You shouldn't let anything stand in the way of your happiness. And if Leo makes you happy, then you must find a way to overcome any obstacles standing in the way, and that includes my brother. Trust me, I wish I'd done that when I was young."

"What do you mean?" Miranda asked.

Aunt Winnie pushed out of her chair. "I mean, my darlings, that I regret not fighting for the man I loved. I don't want you two to regret not finding love. If you don't go after it, you'll both wind up like me—an old maid who still lives with her father and brother."

Bianca saw the sadness in her aunt's eyes. Aunt Winnie was always so cheerful, so positive. But now, Bianca had to wonder what hurts her aunt had hidden behind her serene smiles and her gentle platitudes. Aunt Winnie had a history that she didn't like to discuss, even with her nieces. But she had mentioned a lost love on several occasions. Which made Bianca suspicious of even her dear aunt, too. How many secrets did Aunt Winnie hide, just to protect her brother and father? Or maybe, to protect her nieces? Bianca had never stopped to consider that.

"I'm off to bed," Aunt Winnie said, dismissing the entire subject with a wave of her hand. "You two have a nice visit."

Miranda kissed her aunt good-night. Bianca opened the door for Winnie, then hugged her. "Sleep well."

"At my age, that's debatable," Aunt Winnie said on a soft chuckle.

Bianca waited until her aunt was safely in her bedroom before she turned to face Miranda. "We need to talk."

Miranda gave her a knowing look. "Good. Now you can tell me the real reason you're back here so soon."

Ronald Blanchard glanced in his rearview mirror, making sure for the hundredth time that he wasn't being followed. He turned off Heron Lane and into the dark, wooded area where he was supposed to meet Garret McGraw. Ronald had no intention of paying off the man, but he did want one more chance to convince the P.I. to get out Stoneley. Still not sure how he was going to do this, he was prepared to make a down payment to McGraw, just to stall him.

Careful to guide his SUV up the winding drive to the lookout point in the heart of the park, Ronald begrudged having to drive himself tonight. But this was one trip he had to make alone, in spite of the slick roads and the snow-covered woods.

He reached the treacherous hill leading to the parking area on top of a jagged ridge, then parked the dark SUV and got out, searching in the dark for any sign of the PI. Then he glanced at the dash, quickly switching on an interior light to see the time. It was ten minutes past eight. McGraw was late.

Garrett McGraw groaned as he hurried out of his office. He was late for his appointment with Ronald Blanchard. A last-minute phone call had kept him at the office. Some strange woman asking all kinds of silly questions.

Well, he didn't give out information for free. He'd told the woman he had business to attend to and that she'd have to call back tomorrow.

Only he didn't plan on being in the office tomorrow, or the day after that, or anytime real soon. As soon as he got his money, he was taking off to parts unknown. He'd had enough of Stoneley, Maine. Once, he'd had a future here. Once, he'd been an upstanding citizen of this brutal state, even working as a police officer in Portland. But someone had sold Garrett out, costing him his job.

He'd been forced to come back here and set up shop, barely making ends meet while the mighty Blanchard clan held rein over everything and everyone around.

"Well, that's all about to change," Garrett said to himself as he headed to his car. With thoughts of gulf waters and pretty women in his head, he never saw the dark figure stepping out of the shadows.

And he never saw the blow to his head coming until he felt a sharp pain. Then Garrett McGraw's world went from tropical beaches and sweet-smelling flowers to a cold, black darkness.

"What's wrong?" Miranda asked, her face etched with worry. "Bianca, I know something is up. You'd never leave your job like this to come back home so soon if it wasn't serious. Is it something to do with Leo?"

Bianca motioned toward a chair. "Sit down and I'll explain everything."

Miranda fell back on the ottoman, her hands clasped over her gray sweater.

"I don't know how to begin," Bianca said, wishing there was some other way to do this. She pushed at her hair. "You remember the picture I showed everyone the night of Aunt Winnie's party?"

Miranda nodded. "Mother was in the picture."

"Yes, and we noticed the date on the back. It was dated a week after Mother died, remember?"

"Yes, of course. But we decided that Leo's mom must have been confused with the date."

Bianca leaned forward and took one of Miranda's hands. "She wasn't confused, Miranda. Our mother was with her on that exact date."

Miranda jerked her hand away, gasping. "What are you saying?"

Bianca took another breath. "I think our mother is alive, Miranda. And I think Father knows that. I'm pretty sure he's known all along and he's been hiding it from us."

Miranda got up to pace in front of the fire, a hand to her mouth, her dark ponytail falling past her shoulders. "Bianca, you can't be serious? How can that be?"

"I've found out some things," Bianca began, trying to find a way to explain. "Leo and I—"

"Leo knows about this?"

She nodded as she got up to look out the window. The ocean was as dark and brooding as always, but she could see glittering whitecaps hitting against the rocks below. "I showed the picture to Father and he told me I was just imagining things. He seemed so angry, so shocked. Then I mentioned it to Juliet—"

"How many people know?"

"Just Leo and Juliet right now. But only Leo knows all of it. I was with him most of this weekend."

Miranda stopped pacing, her arms going around her midsection. "With him *where?*"

Bianca explained about the trip to Peoria. "And he went with me to a place in Chicago."

"Chicago? Why did you need to go to Chicago?"

Bianca poured out the whole story then, beginning with hiring Garrett McGraw. She told Miranda everything the P.I. had told her, then explained how she and Leo had gone to the hospital in Chicago. "After he finally let us go, Dr. Brooks refused to tell us who's involved in keeping Mother there, but he practically admitted that she's been a patient all these years. And we found an empty folder with her name on it."

Miranda's shock showed on her pale face. "Why didn't you call someone, the police, anyone?"

"We struck a deal with Dr. Brooks," Bianca explained. "He could have turned us in for trespassing and breaking into the Records room, so we agreed to stay quiet about what we found for now—we needed more time, more evidence. But the doctor is scared. He knows much more than he's saying, and of course, he has patient confidentiality laws on his side. Plus, he claims he has no idea where our mother is."

"But you think she's alive, right?" Miranda asked, her tone full of accusations and disbelief. "You must have some other leads. Or are you hiding something else from me?"

"I've told you everything. Before I bring in the authorities, I have to find more evidence, and we have to find our mother. But believe me, Miranda, she's alive. She's alive and she's out there somewhere. We have to find her soon. She might not be safe."

Miranda looked doubtful, but she grabbed Bianca's arm, holding her there, a look of terror on her face. "You think our father had our mother committed all those years ago? You believe he's been lying to us all this time?"

Bianca could only nod. She swallowed the lump in her throat. "It looks that way. I just need a little more proof. Garrett McGraw is supposed to get back to me with more information. That's why I had to come back." Then she looked into Miranda's red-rimmed eyes. "We have to talk to Father. We have to make him tell us the truth. I'd much rather hear it from him, than through the police."

Miranda started shaking. "I don't think—"

Bianca guided her to the love seat in front of the fire. "I won't leave you alone here. I have to find out the truth."

Miranda looked down at the floor. "But how could our own father do this?"

"I don't know. I just don't know."

Miranda stared into the fire, then looked up. "Should we tell Aunt Winnie?"

"Not just yet," Bianca said. "It would…it would be horrible for her."

"It *is* horrible. For all of us."

Bianca put an arm around her sister's shoulder. "We might have to tell everyone else."

"You mean, our sisters?"

"Yes. I can't stay here indefinitely. Hopefully, Father will confess and we can get on with trying to locate Mother. Leo inadvertently put all of this into motion by giving me that picture. And whoever is helping Father knows about that now—I'm sure Father reported it immediately. They must have moved her right before I showed up at Westside. Now we have to find out where. I'm hoping he will at least help us with that."

Miranda started humming. Bianca recognized it as a lullaby that Trudy used to sing and hum to her daughters to soothe them, especially Miranda.

Bianca didn't stop her sister now. Miranda's shock came as no surprise, and Bianca hated being the one to do this. So she sat silent, her hand in Miranda's and listened as her sister kept humming the sad, haunting tune over and over.

And while she sat, she prayed to God that her mother was safe and warm somewhere far away from the depressing place where Bianca has smelled her perfume.

"Please, God, let it be. Let her be safe." And, Bianca thought, as a tear slid down her face, let her dream good dreams. "We'll bring you home soon, Mother, I promise."

FOURTEEN

An hour later, Bianca rushed down the path to the cliffs, fear making her heart race right along with her feet. Leo had called, asking her to meet him. And he'd specifically asked her to come to the beach. Why down here, she had no idea. But she'd left Miranda waiting in her bedroom, so they could confront Ronald together.

"I'll be back as soon as I find out what's wrong," she'd told her sister. "I need you to be there with me, Miranda, when I talk to Father."

"I'll be waiting," Miranda had said, her eyes blank, her face pale. "I just can't believe this."

Bianca couldn't believe it, either, and she wondered how Ronald would react once they confronted him. Would he keep on denying his involvement? If he did, Bianca would just have to keep digging, even after she got back to Boston. And that would mean bringing in the local police, and alerting the local district attorney. Could she really bring charges against her own father?

Right now, she only wanted to find Leo and hold on to him for a few minutes, at least. He hadn't sounded good on the phone. The urgency in his voice had rattled Bianca.

He was waiting in the shadows just beyond the swing.

"Bianca."

She turned at the sound of his voice carrying over the wind. "Leo, what's going on?"

He pulled her close, engulfing her in the warmth of his heavy wool overcoat. The night was bitterly cold, with a brittle, bone-chilling wind that howled and blew straight off the Atlantic.

Bianca stood back to stare up at him. "You're scaring me. Did Father say something to you?"

Leo quickly shook his head. "No, he avoided me most of the day and I had to deal with one crisis after another, so I didn't get a chance to even speak with him, either. I don't know if I can face him again, knowing the truth."

"Is that why you wanted to meet me down here on the beach instead of in the house?"

He lifted his head toward the house. "That and…something else I just heard."

"What?"

"Bianca, I saw the accident on my way home from working late. I'm so sorry."

Bianca's whole body went rigid. "What accident?"

Leo pushed a hand through his hair. "A car at the

bottom of the ravine on Heron Lane, just past the inn. Traffic was backed up, so I got out to see what had happened."

"Who was it?" she asked, afraid that one of her family members was now dead. "Oh, no. Father?"

"No, I don't know where your father is right now." Leo let out a breath. "It was Garrett McGraw," he said, putting a hand on her cheek. "Your private investigator is dead, Bianca."

Bianca felt sick. "Oh, no, no."

She moaned, then fell against Leo, her head balancing on his chest as he kissed the top of her hair and tried to soothe her by rubbing her back. "I'm sorry."

"Are you sure?" she asked, backing up, hoping she'd heard him wrong. "Leo, did you see him?"

"I didn't have to see him," Leo replied, the grim statement causing Bianca even more shock. "The car crashed and caught on fire. It's crunched like an accordion, but from what I could tell, it was McGraw's car. I asked one of the officers at the scene, a friend of mine, and he told me off the record, they'd identified the man as Garrett McGraw and that the man was dead."

Bianca's knees seemed to turn to water. "Did they say—I mean, it was an accident, right?"

Leo looked out toward the foaming water. "They seem to think so, but that's why I wanted to see you." He lifted her head, so she'd look at him. "*I* don't think it was an accident. It's too much of a coincidence."

Bianca's shock now turned to anger. "I think you're right. Somebody must have run Garrett off that road."

"Maybe the same someone who tried to run you down a couple of times."

She stood there, the sound of wind and water echoing through her mind, thinking that this was her home. As gloomy as this big, old house seemed at times, and even with the questions surrounding her mother's death, Bianca had always felt reasonably safe here at Blanchard Mansion. But that had changed now. Tonight, she felt vulnerable and afraid, disoriented. Someone wanted to keep her mother dead. And that same someone might want the same thing for Bianca.

She looked up at Leo, her heart brimming with an intense pain. "Do you think my own father would try to have me killed, Leo?"

He pulled her back into his arms. "No, I don't believe Ronald would go that far. But we can't be sure, can we?" He kissed her, his lips touching her cold cheek. "I don't want to let you out of my sight."

"You can't watch over me day and night."

"I just had to see you, to make sure you were all right."

She stared up at the house. "But not inside the mansion. You're afraid someone might be watching and listening, right?"

She felt his movement. "Yes."

"I have to confront my father," she said, her resolve overcoming her fears. "That's the only way. Maybe if he hears that McGraw is dead, he'll realize this has gotten too dangerous. Whoever is behind everything won't have any qualms about doing away with my mother for good this time."

"Or you," Leo reminded her. "I'll go with you to talk to him."

"No, you can't," she said. "I won't let you. It's enough that you're already involved. You risked a lot by helping me in Chicago. I won't allow you to…put yourself in that position again."

He stepped back and looked up at the house. Then he searched her face, his eyes touching on her, holding her. "Bianca, there's so much…I need to say."

She stopped him with a finger on his lips. "Not now. Not tonight. I have to talk to my father. Once I find out what he knows, I'll go from there."

"And where do I fit in, once this is over?"

She couldn't answer that. "I don't know. I know I want you in my life. But I have to be sure."

"About your father? Or about me?"

"I have to be sure I'm ready for…everything we could have together."

"What if I told you I'm ready now?"

"Don't," she said. "Don't—not just yet. I don't want to remember this night in that way. Garrett McGraw is dead, and I have to put my sister through the horror of going to my father with everything I know."

"We'll probably never know what McGraw had, all the evidence he found," Leo pointed out.

Bianca stared up at the house. A light shone in her father's downstairs study. "Someone knew. And maybe that's why he was killed." Then she put her hands on his arms. "I don't want to have to worry about you, too, not tonight."

Leo tugged her into his embrace, his kiss telling her what she needed to know. "I want this to be over," he whispered. "I want us to be together."

"Me, too," she replied. "Soon, I hope. Maybe Father will tell me the truth and I can find my mother. If he'll just be honest with me, I can try to forgive him. I want my mother back. I want my family healed and together, whole again." Then she touched a hand to Leo's face. "Until then, I can't…be sure what will come next."

Leo held her there in his arms, the soft moonlight shadowing his face with longing and regret. "Remember our promise. No matter what—"

"I will," she said. But he looked so intense, his expression holding so many secrets, that she repeated it to him. "No matter what, Leo."

"And that means no matter what you find out from your father tonight, okay?"

"Okay."

He kissed her again, the warmth of his touch

bringing her the courage she needed to face her father. Then he walked her up the rugged, curving path to the back of the house. "I don't want to leave you. I could camp out in the yard."

"You'd freeze."

"I could stay in the garage."

"No. This is my home. My father wouldn't dare try anything in his own house."

"I don't like this. Maybe I can just hide out in a spare bedroom."

"I'll be fine. I'll have Miranda nearby, and Aunt Winnie. We have a security system and a staff that never seems to sleep. I'll be careful."

"Call me later," he said. "Call me after you talk to Ronald and let me know you're all right. I don't care how late it is."

"I will. I'll need to hear your voice." She looked up at the light in Miranda's room. "I have to go. I left Miranda alone and she's very upset. I need to get back to her so we can get this over with."

Leo kissed her one last time. She sensed he wanted to say more, but Bianca didn't want to ruin what she felt with Leo by giving in to her feelings on such a terrible night. Whatever she'd set into motion, she had to see through. Garrett McGraw was dead. Who might be next? The urgency of the situation only added to her sense of being watched. She didn't know who she could trust anymore.

Leo must have felt the tension. He held her close. "Are you going to be all right?"

"I have to. Miranda needs me to be strong." She hugged him against her one last time. "Maybe it will all be over tonight, once we talk to Father."

"I hope so," Leo said. "You'll call me, remember?"

"I will."

"And…we'll figure out what to do."

"Soon," she said, pulling away, her hand trailing in his.

"No matter what," he reminded her.

"No matter what."

She hurried inside the house, then turned and watched through the beveled glass of the back door as he disappeared on the path.

Ronald glanced up, surprise masking his face, as Bianca and Miranda came into his study. After making sure no one was lurking about in the hallway, Bianca carefully shut the heavy pocket doors behind her and surveyed her father's sanctuary. The room was huge and dark, masculine in its severity, with a big fireplace where a crackling fire tried valiantly to put some warmth out into the shadowy recesses of the paneled walls.

"I'm here, ladies," Ronald said from behind his desk. "Bianca, it's late. What was so urgent that it couldn't wait until morning?"

Bianca could see the lines of fatigue around her

father's eyes. And she could see the apprehension and doubt in his expression. He was as terrified as she. "We need to talk to you," she said, taking Miranda by the arm to lead her to a black leather wing chair.

"I can see that," Ronald said. "Miranda, why are you staring at me like that?"

Bianca glanced over at her sister. Miranda's eyes were red rimmed and wide, her expression full of shock and mistrust. Holding a steadying arm on Miranda, Bianca said, "Father, I need to talk to you and I asked Miranda to come with me. She doesn't want to be here."

Ronald looked at his Rolex. "Well, neither do I. It's been a long day."

Bianca sat up in her chair. "Then I'll get right to the point. Do you know where our mother is?"

Ronald immediately became agitated. "Bianca, is that what this is about? You know the answer to that!" He waved a hand toward Miranda. "No wonder you don't want to be here. This is ridiculous!" He started up out of his chair, but Bianca's next words brought him back to his seat.

"Garrett McGraw is dead, Father. He died in a car accident tonight just off Heron Lane. It seems the roads around here are treacherous, even after all this time."

"What?" Ronald went pale, but he quickly recovered. "Who is Garrett McGraw?"

"He was the private investigator I hired to research Mother's death, but then, you already know that, don't you?"

Ronald sat quietly for a minute, his eyes downcast, his hands on the desk. "I don't know what you're implying, Bianca, but you are way off course here. Your mother is dead. How many times do I have to repeat that?"

"Did she *really* die that night, Father?" Miranda asked, her quiet words causing Ronald to flinch away. "Just tell us the truth, so we can figure out what to do. We'll find a way to get through this."

"What is there to *do?*" Ronald asked, beating a hand on the desk. "What is there to say? She's dead. Her car plunged off that cliff. I'm telling you the truth. She's dead to me."

Bianca sat forward, her own fist pounding on the desk. "You had the body cremated in another town, Father. Why would you do that?"

Ronald sliced a hand through his dark hair. "I was in anguish. I wasn't thinking straight."

Bianca watched that anguish now as it twisted her father's face. "I can believe that. You were in anguish because you were lying. And you've been lying for twenty-three years. But why? What did Mother do to make you turn on her like that? What could she have done to make you lock her away?"

"Lock her away?"

For the first time, Bianca saw complete and

genuine shock on her father's face. "I believe she's been kept against her will, probably sedated, at a medical retreat near Chicago. And don't tell me you know nothing about this. You know. You're probably paying the bill. McGraw must have stumbled on something really incriminating for you to have him killed."

"I did not have that man, whoever he is—was—killed. And I don't know what you're talking about."

Bianca didn't let up. "You sent our mother away. That much is true, isn't it?"

Ronald got up, stomped behind his chair. The glow of the fire cast his face in pale golden shadows. "She was leaving me, Bianca. Can't you understand how upset I was that night? Your mother was *leaving me.*"

Bianca glanced over at Miranda. Her sister was quietly sobbing, her hand on her mouth. "So you had her killed for that?" Miranda managed to ask.

"I didn't have her killed," Ronald shouted. "I didn't! She left and then, it was over."

"No, it is not over, because she's still alive," Bianca said, pushing words at him as if he were on the witness stand, which he was in her mind. "You sent her away, but you told us she was dead. Maybe to protect us, maybe to spare us the pain of your separation. But can't you see we've all suffered enough? Can't you trust us enough to tell us the truth?"

Ronald hit his hand against an exquisite porcelain vase, sending it shattering to the floor behind his desk. "Your mother is dead, Bianca. And you should let her rest in peace."

"I can't," Bianca said, both hands on the desk now. "I can't do that, Father. I have to go back to Boston, to work. I've already taken too much time and I have a big case coming up. But I want you to know and understand, I am not going to give up on this. I'll keep digging, and I'll hire every P.I. in the state of Maine, if I have to, to get answers. If you don't tell me what I need to know, then I'll have to go to the authorities and see if I can build a case that way.

"I know my mother is alive. You kept her in that horrid place in Chicago, in a padded room. I can't prove it, but I'll keep working until I do. You had to have help. Someone is in on this with you. I believe that *someone* killed Garrett McGraw because he was getting too close to the truth. And I believe you know exactly who that person is."

Ronald's face was red with rage and fear now. "What are you talking about? What place in Chicago?"

For the first time, Bianca saw real confusion on her father's face. "Westside Medical Retreat," she said. "You know the place. It's a medical facility for mentally disturbed patients. Is that why you kept mother a secret all these years, because she's so sick?"

Ronald turned to touch a hand to the bookshelf behind his desk, using it for support as he drew in long, deep breaths. "I don't know what you're talking about, Bianca. Honestly, I don't."

Bianca motioned to Miranda. Miranda got up, still shaken, still silently sobbing.

Bianca, however, continued to drive her point home. "Father, I can't make you confess, and I don't have enough proof to go forward with this, especially since Garrett McGraw is dead now. But I'll keep trying to find evidence. I'm going to find my mother and I'm going to bring her home."

Ronald turned to face them, anger and revulsion coloring his features. "Did Leo put you up to this?"

"Leo?" Bianca cast a glance at Miranda. Her sister looked as shocked as she felt. "Why would you ask that?"

"He gave you that picture. I told you he did it deliberately. But did he tell you why he sought you out in the first place?"

Bianca's heart lurched at the vengeful glee on her father's face. "He wanted to get to know me better. We've become close, in spite of your threats to fire him."

Ronald actually laughed. "Is that what he told you? That'd I'd fire him if he didn't leave you alone?"

Bianca nodded, holding on to Miranda for support. "Didn't you threaten him?"

Ronald regained his composure, his tight grin full of triumph. "I told him I'd fire him if he *didn't* win you over. Bianca, darling, you've been hounding me for answers, thinking I'm deceitful, but *I'm* not the one deceiving you. I ordered Leo to convince you to come back to work for me at Blanchard Fabrics. That's been my only goal since you went to Boston. And Leo's only goal was to do my bidding. If you think that man actually has feelings for you, then you are sorely mistaken."

He pushed his chair under the desk, then stalked to the door, turning to face Bianca and Miranda. "And you're accusing *me* of lying? You might want to ask Leo why he'd give you a picture that is clearly marked wrong, knowing that would only stir up trouble in this family? Why would he do such a cruel thing, to you, to all of us? Ask him that, and then make *him* tell you the truth."

Bianca heard the doors shutting, heard the fire's hissing and popping. Then she heard her sister's gentle urgings. "Come on, let's get you upstairs."

But she couldn't move. She couldn't breathe. Her mind was reeling, reliving every conversation, every quiet moment she'd had with Leo. Had it all been part of the lies? Had he given her the picture as a means of getting closer to her, a means of helping her out, so she'd become indebted to him, endeared to him? So she'd turn to him, only him? It couldn't be true, could it?

"Bianca, please," Miranda said, tugging her toward the door. "You're about to collapse."

Bianca felt the tremors in her body just before

Miranda grabbed her and helped her sink down into a chair. "Why would Leo do that?" she asked, her voice faraway and husky in her own ears. "Why would he make me believe he loved me, when all this time he's been…lying? Miranda, what's happening to me? What if Father is right?"

Miranda held Bianca's hands tightly in her own. "Father is just trying to hurt you, don't you see that? If Leo did this, then it's because Father forced him to do so, Bianca. That has to be it."

Because she couldn't bear that, Bianca crumbled over, her head in her hands, her tears coming from fatigue and confusion and, now, betrayal.

And she remembered Leo's plea to her earlier. "No matter what."

He'd been trying to tell her, all along he'd been trying to warn her, but she'd been too caught up in finding her mother to listen, to see what had been right before her eyes.

And now, she could never forgive Leo.

No matter what.

It was Miranda's turn to comfort her sister. And she did. She pulled Bianca into her arms and rocked her back and forth as they both cried there in the dark study, while the fire hissed and laughed.

Bianca held tightly to her sister while the old mansion held tightly to its secret.

FIFTEEN

Early the next morning, Leo came to Blanchard Manor, intent on making sure Bianca was all right.

She hadn't called him last night.

And she wasn't answering her cell phone.

He'd even called the main line to the house, but was told that Miss Blanchard had left instructions that she wasn't to be disturbed.

Something wasn't right.

Leo jabbed a finger against the intricately scrolled brass doorbell box, waiting for someone to answer. Sonya the dour-faced housekeeper opened the door, her dark eyes evaluating him with a frown. "May I help you?"

"I need to see Bianca."

Sonya shook her head. "She doesn't want to see anyone."

"Tell her it's Leo."

She gave him another frown, then said, "I'll be right back." Then she shut the door in his face.

Wondering what to do, and imagining all sorts of bad scenarios, Leo paced back and forth on the aged stone portico. When the door creaked opened again, he breathed a sigh of relief. Until he saw Miranda standing there.

"Miranda, hi. Where's Bianca?"

Miranda tugged her heavy brown button-up sweater over her white blouse, then came out and shut the door. "Leo, Bianca isn't feeling well this morning. I think it would be best if you just go."

Leo stared at Miranda, taking in the dark circles of fatigue around her eyes. She looked as if she hadn't slept very much, either. "Is she all right?" he asked, running a hand through his hair. "I mean, how did your father react to everything?"

"Not very well," Miranda said, her words just above a whisper. "This has been difficult for all of us. We're still in shock."

"Did he admit the truth?"

Miranda had just opened her mouth to respond when the door banged back. Ronald stood there, his gaze sweeping over Leo, his glare as gray and frosty as the morning fog coming in off the water. "Get away from my daughter," he said. "Get out of here, and stay away, Leo. I mean it."

Miranda rushed to Ronald. "Father, let's just go back inside."

"Not until I personally see him off the premises," Ronald said, his expression wild with anger. He looked unkempt and disoriented, a man far removed from the cool, calm executive Leo had once admired.

Leo's heart hammered a warning against his rib cage. "Where's Bianca?"

Ronald let out a little chuckle, then flapped his hands in the air as if to shoo Leo away. "Packing to go back to Boston, I imagine. She's leaving, Leo. And she wants no part of you. You have failed at your mission. Which means I no longer need your services at Blanchard Fabrics, either."

Leo shook his head, then looked down. "No, you don't get to fire me. I quit." He didn't care about his job, but he did care about Bianca. "Now tell me, what did you do to her?"

"Me?" Ronald shouted, pointing a finger at Leo. "I didn't do anything. But you, you poisoned her against me. You showed her that picture and got her started on this wild-goose chase to find her mother. You turned her against me, and for that, I will never, ever forgive you."

Leo lunged toward Ronald. "I didn't have to do that. She figured things out about you all on her own."

Ronald started for Leo, but Miranda pushed between them. "Stop it. Father, stop it." Then she turned to Leo. "Please, just go."

"I can't," he said. "Not without Bianca."

Ronald beat a hand against the door. "Bianca knows, Leo. She knows what you were doing. I told her all about our little plan. And believe me, she doesn't want to see you. Ever again."

Leo's world shifted with all the power of an earthquake. Bianca knew the truth. Ronald had told her the truth, and knowing Ronald, he'd taken a perverse pleasure in doing so. "You had to get even, didn't you?" he asked Ronald, his voice husky and low. "You had to break her heart, because she got too close to the truth."

"The truth?" Ronald growled. "The truth is that you are the one who broke her heart. You're the one who betrayed her. She doesn't love you, Leo. You couldn't even succeed at making that happen. Just leave before I call the police to escort you off my property."

Leo couldn't put a name to his despair. The pain of losing Bianca stabbed at him with sharp-edged precision. He had to find her and make her see that he loved her. That he had never meant to hurt her. But how?

He turned to Miranda. "Is she gone?"

Miranda glanced at Ronald, then looked back at Leo, her expression laced with sympathy. "No, but she will be soon." She touched a hand to Leo's sleeve. "Give her some time, Leo. She's been through so much."

Leo couldn't do that. He couldn't waste any more time. He'd already made a mess of things by holding back the truth from Bianca. He should have been honest with her the very first night. Now, it was too late and he didn't have the luxury of time.

But right now, he did need to take care of some things. He had to make arrangements to get to Boston. He was going to find Bianca before the day was over. And somehow, he was going to find a way to make her understand and forgive him.

No matter what.

Upstairs in the turret room, Bianca had watched the whole scene below from behind a lacy curtain. Now she stood there, her fingers clutching the sheer fabric, as Leo turned to get in his car. But just before he did so, he looked up to where she stood. Bianca couldn't move, so she stared down at him, her whole body shattered by an intense pain.

Leo held her gaze for a minute, his expression etched in that same pain, as if he were trying to send her a silent plea to forgive him. Then he got in his car and drove away.

In his study, Ronald sat with his head between his hands, tears forming in his eyes as he stared down at the aged wedding picture of himself and Trudy. She was so beautiful, so fragile, like a beautiful doll all dressed up in white lace and fine silk. He ran a finger over her image, wishing for so many things.

"I'm so sorry," he said, his heart heavy with remorse. "So very sorry. Not only for what I've done to you, but for the pain I've caused Bianca and Miranda, too."

He was still sitting there, staring at the picture, when Alannah sauntered into the room, dressed in cream and black, her heavy fur wrap tossed over her shoulder. "Ronald, I called work and they told me you were still here. Are you feeling all right, darling?"

Ronald quickly put the picture in his desk drawer, then rubbed at his eyes. "I'm tired, Alannah. Just so very tired."

"Oh, my poor baby," Alannah said, rushing to put her arms around his neck. "I can't wait for our trip to Europe. You really need a good, long rest. This place is so depressing." She kissed him. "We're going to have such an adventure, I promise—I've booked all the best hotels. I'll take care of you. Don't worry. You *will* have a good time, and very sweet dreams." As she stood behind him, cooing, Ronald was overcome by her strong, spicy perfume.

But he could only smell the scent of roses and jasmine.

And he could only hear his beautiful Trudy telling him, "'To sleep, perchance to dream.'"

Bianca glanced around the shadowy darkness of her brownstone. It seemed so empty and cold. Shivering, she hurried to turn on lamps, then checked the thermostat to make sure the heat was up high enough.

After dropping her bags in her bedroom, she got

into a comfortable pair of baby-blue velour sweatpants and matching hooded jacket, hoping the soft material would bring her the warmth she craved.

But then, she didn't think she'd ever stop shivering. She'd been cold and numb on the drive back from Stoneley, but it wasn't just from the frigid late January weather.

Her heart was shattered, broken like brittle ice. Broken into a million little jagged pieces.

She stood at the kitchen counter, waiting for the bright red kettle to heat up some water for tea. Maybe a soothing cup of chamomile would help. As the kettle started whistling, Bianca pulled it off the burner, then set it back down on the stove. Her hands were shaking as she fought against the tears welling in her eyes again.

"They both betrayed me," she said out loud, her voice raw with pain and emotion. "First my father, and now Leo."

She automatically placed a tea bag in one of the dainty floral cups Aunt Winnie had given her last Christmas, then carried the cup and saucer into the sitting area. Dropping onto the creamy yellow chaise longue by the window, she admired the glowing gaslights of Boston's Beacon Hill.

She should be relieved to be home. But her mind couldn't find any rest. Her mother was still out there somewhere, alone and afraid, and Bianca couldn't live with her own failure. Garrett McGraw was dead, and it was probably because he'd been working for her. And her own father was lying to her, for reasons she might not ever know or understand.

And then, there was Leo.

Leo. She put her head back against the soft suede of the chaise, closing her eyes to remember everything about Leo. That first night—had he purposely sought her out just to please her father?

She could see it all so clearly now. He'd even teased her about that very thing. Maybe even then, he had been trying to tell her the truth. But why hadn't he? He'd had so many opportunities to be open and honest with her. She'd asked him over and over if Ronald was threatening him.

And he had told her he could handle Ronald.

Maybe he'd believed that, but her father was too powerful, too ruthless, for Leo to take on alone. Maybe he'd tried, really tried, to stop what her father had put into motion, but he'd waited too late to be honest with Bianca. Did he keep the truth from her because he wanted to protect her, or was he just trying to protect himself?

"If you'd only told me," she said now, the silence of being alone singing inside her brain. "If only you'd trusted me, Leo."

She took a sip of her tea, then noticed the phone centered on the table by the chaise. The message light was blinking. Sure that she had several messages from work, Bianca hit the button to listen.

Three messages from her assistant. Two from one of the paralegals helping her with her next case. Both urgent. Then one that surprised and touched her. It was from Miranda.

"Hi. Listen, I'm just so worried about you. Call me and let me know you made it home okay. Oh, and I'm also worried about Leo. Father tried to fire him this morning, but Leo quit. I think he's on his way to find you. And…I think you should give him another chance."

"Another chance?" Bianca said, jabbing the delete button on the answering machine. Why should she give Leo another chance, after the way he'd withheld something so deceitful and devious from her?

Because you love him, her conscience prodded. *And because he tried to tell you. He tried, but you were too caught up in all the mystery and intrigue surrounding your mother.*

"No matter what," she said, tears brimming again. "No matter what."

He'd urged her to remember that. But did that include him trying to trick her into falling for him, just so he could win points with her father by bringing her back to Blanchard Fabrics?

Feeling sick to her stomach, Bianca got up to pour out her lukewarm tea. Then she called Miranda, assuring her sister that she was okay. After that, she simply sat and stared into space. It was late and she should go to bed, but she knew she wouldn't sleep.

Regardless, she had to get to work early tomorrow to make up for lost time. At least she'd have something to focus on. She could block all the ugliness out by pouring herself into this important case.

But would she be able to block out Leo's kisses or his promises, his smile, his ability to make her laugh and feel safe? How was she supposed to forget all of that?

She closed her eyes, her prayers silent and simple. *What plans do You have for me, Lord? Was all of this just some silly dream? Why can't I find my mother? And why does it hurt so much to love Leo?*

Help me to forget him, Lord. Help me to...forget that I love him.

He wouldn't let her forget him.

Leo got out of the rental car and stood at the curb in front of Bianca's brownstone. It hadn't been hard to find the address and it hadn't taken him long to get from the airport to here. But now that he was here, he had to stop and catch his breath.

He was so nervous, so afraid that she'd turn him away, he felt as if he might not be able to breathe. His chest hurt, a great vise of regret and defeat weighing at it. His head hurt from wondering why he hadn't done the right thing from the very beginning. He'd prayed on the quick flight here, told God every little thing that was bothering him, asked God to forgive him for every big transgression he'd committed in the past. But especially, for hurting Bianca. Too little, too late, he thought. He doubted God was listening to his pleas. But he wasn't leaving until *Bianca* at least listened to him.

He mustered up his courage and rushed up the steps to the front door of her quaint brownstone. Then he rang the bell, said a prayer for guidance, and waited for her to come to the door.

Bianca jumped up, her head crashing against the back of the chaise. She must have drifted off to sleep after all. Someone was ringing the doorbell. And she had a pretty good idea of who that someone was.

Leo.

Should she just ignore him?

Her head told her to do that, but her heart was beating way too fast to listen to her head. Still shaky, she pushed off the chaise and went to the door. At first, she leaned against it, listening to the fist pounding on the other side. Listening to Leo.

"Bianca, I know you're in there. I need to talk to you. You have every right to hate me. I don't blame you for that. But…you need to know something. I *love* you. Do you hear me? I love you."

She heard him. Fresh tears misted her eyes. She heard him, but how could she trust him?

He pounded once more, then started talking again, his voice low but firm. "At first, I agreed with your father. I told him I'd try to win you over, so you'd come back to Blanchard Fabrics. But that was before I looked into your eyes that night at the party. What I never told you, what I could never say, was this. Something changed that night, while we were out on the beach. I think I fell for you. Right there. Right then. And after that, things got so confusing, with all this about your mother. I had to protect you. I still want to protect you. But I never meant to hurt you. Remember, no matter what? Bianca?"

She leaned against the door, her warm forehead pressed against the cool wood. And she thought about everything Leo had brought into her life—his warmth, his smile, his ability to make her feel safe, even when locked in a dank, dark room. He'd even brought God back into her life, during one of the worst times of her life. And he'd done all of that—stood by her—even while risking the wrath of her father.

Leo had told her he'd be with her, no matter what. And he'd tried so very hard to keep that promise.

Bianca touched the door, closed her eyes, and said a prayer. Then she whispered, "No matter what," and she opened the door.

A look of relief and surprise on his face, Leo rushed inside, slamming the door behind him as he pulled her into his arms. "No matter what."

But Bianca needed more before she took the final step. She needed to hear it from him, all of it. She pushed her hands to his chest and backed away.

"You were trying to tell me. Every time we were together, you tried to warn me, didn't you?"

He bobbed his head. "Yes, I did. But I was a coward. I couldn't find the right time. You had so much going on, and after a while, my only thought was that I had to protect you, even from my own betrayal."

"But you stuck with me. You helped me, even when it meant my father would turn on you."

He nodded again. "He did threaten to fire me. He didn't want me to *love* you. He only wanted me to use you. I kept telling him I couldn't do it. But I couldn't tell him that I loved you so much, it hurt. I couldn't risk making him even more angry, at you, at us."

Bianca could understand his predicament. But it still hurt. "Why didn't you explain everything to me, Leo?"

He touched a hand to her face. "Would you have listened? I think you would have turned me away, and then you'd have gone off on your own to Chicago. I couldn't let that happen. I'm so sorry that I didn't tell you, so sorry that I wound up doing the one thing I tried to avoid—hurting you. I wanted to tell you when we were at my sister's, but…I needed to keep you safe."

"So you lied to protect me?"

"I never lied. I just never told you everything."

"And that's supposed to justify this?"

"No, nothing can make this right. But all the way

here, I prayed to God to help me, to help us, through this. I asked His forgiveness, but I really need you to forgive me, too. I'm here for the long haul, Bianca. I want to be with you. I want to help you find your mother. I want to love you."

Bianca knew she wasn't thinking straight. So much had happened. She should send him away, should tell him to never bother her again. But she also knew that she needed him, so much. She didn't want to be alone anymore. She wanted to believe Leo could make a difference in her life.

"What about my father?" she asked.

"I quit. I was going to anyway. I can't work for him anymore. And...I've always liked Boston. Maybe it's time for me to move here. We could start over, together, and away from your father."

"But he can still make things very difficult for us."

"We'll find a way around him, I promise."

She could see the promise in his eyes. "No matter what?"

"No matter what."

She leaned against the wall, her head down. "The night my mother left, she quoted something to me from Shakespeare's *Hamlet.* She kissed me and said, 'Go to sleep, my sweet Bianca. Everything will be all right in the morning.' Then she said, 'To sleep, perchance to dream.'" Bianca looked up at the man she loved and smiled. "Now I understand what she meant."

Leo reached for her again, his eyes as misty as her own. "She wanted you to be safe and warm and happy, with no bad dreams. She wanted you to live. Just live."

Bianca rushed into his arms, her fears evaporating into a sweet mist of remembrance as her mother's comforting image floated through her mind. "Yes," she said. "Yes, she did. I love you. If nothing else, this quest to find my mother brought us together."

"I love you, too." Leo kissed her then, showing her that dreams could be sweet and safe and comforting, and that they could come true. "I'll be with you," he said. "Always."

Bianca again heard the echo of that same promise from God, too. And she knew that with God's grace and Leo's love, she would find her mother. Somehow.

EPILOGUE

The woman pulled the red cashmere scarf around her blond, disheveled hair, her dark sunglasses shielding her from the early-morning sunshine and any curious observers on the train who might want to make conversation. She didn't want to talk to anyone right now. Maybe not ever again. An image of pain and torment flashed through her mind, but she quickly pushed it away.

With an unsteady hand, she pulled a crumpled picture out of the pocket of her trench coat, then stared down at the handsome man. He looked so scholarly, so distinguished in this photo she'd found in an old university directory. Even though he'd obviously aged, he was just as she remembered. And she had to find him.

It would be a long trip across the country. But then, she needed the time. To think. To plan. And to seek the help she needed, at last. As the train started clattering away from the station, she leaned her head back and tried to imagine what she would find once she reached California.

She hoped she'd find someone to hold her, to remember her, to help her. She hoped she'd find some peace at last.

Then she looked out the window, the bittersweet images in her mind rolling away while the snow-covered countryside slid by in a white-soft mist of longing.

"'Such is the stuff of dreams,'" she whispered, a single teardrop rolling down her face.

* * * * *

Dear Reader,

Don't you just love a good gothic tale? *Fatal Image* is definitely that. But this tale involves more than just a spooky mansion and lots of intrigue. THE SECRETS OF STONELEY series also involves a deep, abiding faith element that tempers all the strange happenings at Blanchard Manor. I thoroughly enjoyed writing about Bianca and Leo, even though I had to guide them through some heavy troubles.

But then, isn't that what faith is all about? God is there with us in the deepest, darkest hours of the night. He is our refuge against fears and doubts, and even when we have nightmares instead of sweet dreams, He is there each day to help us start over. Life can be like that sometimes—good and sweet, or scary and dangerous. Either way, the Lord is our protector. Even when we are seized by fear and trembling, we have only to call out to God and we will be safe, no matter the situation.

I hope this story inspires you to find comfort and courage through your faith. And I invite you to follow the continuing story of THE SECRETS OF STONELEY in the wonderful tales that will follow mine. Look for them in your favorite bookstore.

Until next time, may the angels watch over you—always.

Lenora Worth

QUESTIONS FOR DISCUSSION

1. Why did Bianca dread being back at Blanchard Manor? Have you ever been away from your family because of past conflicts?

2. Leo started out with a deception. How did he resolve this in his mind? Have you ever deceived someone and regretted it? How did you make amends?

3. Why did Bianca have such a strong belief that her mother was still alive? Do you believe in following your instincts in times of doubt?

4. How did the close bond between Bianca and her sister help her in this situation? Do you find that family ties always overcome bad times?

5. What happened to make Leo change his tactics toward Bianca? Do you believe he handled things properly? Do you think it's wise to withhold information to protect someone you care about?

6. How did Bianca go about finding out the truth? Why do you think Ronald denied his part in her mother's death?

7. Do you think Trudy is alive? Do you believe that determination is a gift or a curse? How can being determined in your life help toward building your faith?

8. Leo and Bianca both had to go on trust and instincts, even at the end when Bianca found out the truth. How did this change the dynamics of their relationship? Do you go on faith, or do you need proof to back things up?

Stoneley police detective Mick Campbell has been assigned to investigate Garrett McGraw's suspicious death—and finds himself bumping heads with Portia Blanchard. Portia's only trying to protect her family, but Mick wants to know all the secrets she's hiding. Find out what this Blanchard sister learns about her family history in Shirlee McCoy's LITTLE GIRL LOST....

And now, turn the page for a sneak preview of LITTLE GIRL LOST, the second installment of The Secrets of Stoneley. On sale February from Steeple Hill Books.

Detective Mick Campbell followed the sound of laughter across a road and through a cove of trees. Unless he missed his guess, the pond he was looking for was just ahead. According to Winnie Blanchard, all six of the Blanchard sisters were skating there. A thin layer of snow muffled his footsteps as he stepped into a clearing shadowed in twilight. The pond, much larger than Mick had expected, shimmered in the fading light. As Winnie had said, six women were in the center of the ice. Five stood with their backs to Mick. The sixth sat in a puddle of bright fabric, laughing up at her sisters. Mick had the impression of wide, dark eyes, finely drawn features, and curly hair pulled back from a pale face.

Which sister was she? Not Miranda. Mick had known the eldest of the six in high school, and had seen her once since his return to Stoneley nine months before. Bright colors weren't her style.

Neither was loud laughter. If memory served, Juliet had fair hair and light eyes. He'd seen pictures of Bianca in recent weeks. This wasn't her. That left Cordelia and the twins—Nerissa and Portia.

The woman sitting on the ice laughed again, extending her hand to one of the other women and allowing herself to be pulled upright. Perhaps she sensed his gaze. One minute she was laughing, the next she fell silent. Even from a distance Mick could see her body stiffen, her back straighten. She turned her head, glancing up the slope of the hill to where he stood.

He raised a hand in greeting and strode forward, not quite catching what she said to her sisters. Whatever it was had them turning as one to watch his approach.

"Hello. Can we help you?" she called out to him, gliding forward a few inches before slipping and landing in a heap on the ice once again. This time she didn't laugh, though Mick was sure she wanted to.

"I'm Detective Mick Campbell. Stoneley Police Department."

"What can we do for you, Detective?" She struggled to her feet as her sisters started toward the edge of the pond.

"I'm investigating the death of Garrett McGraw. I've got a few questions I'd like to ask your family."

"According to the newspaper, McGraw was drunk and drove off a cliff. I don't see what that has to do with us." Bianca Blanchard stepped from the ice and sat on a wood bench, her dark eyes calm as she undid her skates.

"McGraw was dead before his car went over the cliff."

"Heart attack?" Bianca pulled on boots and stood.

"He was murdered." Mick watched for a reaction, scanning the faces of each of the sisters, hoping to glimpse guilt or innocence in their expressions. His attention was caught and held by the only sister still on ice. She moved gingerly, wobbling on skates she obviously wasn't used to, her brow creased with concentration. Unlike her sisters, she lacked a natural grace on ice, though her quiet beauty and guarded expression made Mick want to look closer.

"Murdered? Are you sure?" Bianca spoke, pulling Mick's attention back to the conversation.

"Unfortunately." Things would have been easier if the answer had been a different one. A man like McGraw made as many enemies as he did friends. Finding the person responsible for his death might prove difficult, though Mick was determined to do so. He owed his ex-partner that much.

"And you think this has something to do with our family?" It was Miranda who spoke this time, her concern obvious.

"Your father and aunt are waiting at the house. Why don't we discuss it there?"

"Why don't you tell us what you suspect? Then maybe we'll talk." Another one of the sisters spoke, her short hair spiking out from under the knit cap she wore.

"Because the house is a much warmer place to talk, Delia." Miranda pushed her feet into black snow boots. "I, for one, could use a cup of coffee."

"Coffee would be good. Are you okay, Portia?" Bianca grabbed her skates and turned toward the pond. Mick followed the direction of her gaze, saw the skirt-wearing sister still easing toward the edge of the ice.

"I'm fine. Just give me another minute."

Portia. He should have known. The name fit the woman, its exotic sound matching her interesting choice of clothes. Despite three years spent avoiding women and relationships, Mick was intrigued. As he watched, she stepped off the pond, her feet wobbling, her focus on her sisters rather than the ground. He knew what would happen next, and moved toward her.

A few questions he wanted to ask the family? The detective made it sound so innocuous, his relaxed manner belying the seriousness of what was happening. Obviously, if he didn't suspect her family was involved in McGraw's murder, Detective Campbell wouldn't be here. Portia tried to silently convey her fear to her sisters, but they all seemed intent on grabbing skates and moving toward the path that led back to Blanchard Manor. She'd have to say something. That was all there was to it. I—"

Before she could finish, her ankle twisted under her and she tripped, bracing herself for the third fall of the evening. Instead, hard fingers gripped her arm, pulling her upright. "Whoa! Careful."

"Thanks." Portia looked up into clear blue eyes and a face as cold and implacable as Maine in the winter. She didn't know what she'd been hoping for—compassion? Softness? Some sign that he wasn't here to destroy her family? It wasn't there. All she saw was determination and an anger that burned beneath his cool gaze.

"No problem." He stepped back, putting distance between them, though he watched her intently, as if waiting for her to stumble again. She hoped she'd disappoint him, but the skates twisted as she took an unsteady step toward the bench.

He grabbed her arm again, "Keep it up and you'll break your ankle."

"It wouldn't be the first time."

He stared into her eyes for a moment, then smiled, the slow upward curve of his lips causing her heart to stall and start up again.

"Why doesn't that surprise me?"

"Because you've seen how graceful I am?'

"Let me help you, Portia." Rissa grabbed her hand, squeezing twice, the silent communication they'd perfected as children and still used on occasion. *What are you doing?*

What *was* she doing? Her family might be in serious trouble, the business her grandfather had worked so hard for, in for more of the bad publicity it had garnered a few weeks ago. This wasn't a good time to be joking with a man whose motives weren't clear. Especially not when that man seemed determined to dig up more trouble for her family.

She shot a look at her twin, shrugged her shoulder in response to her questioning look and hurried over to the bench, trying her best to ignore the detective as she fought with the laces on her skates. Unfortunately, he was hard to ignore, his presence a disturbing note to the already discordant evening, his intense stare making her fingers fumble on the laces.

Exasperated, she looked up at him. "You're welcome to head back to the house if I'm taking too long, Detective."

"I've got plenty of time." A half smile eased some of the intensity from his face, and Portia found herself studying the craggy planes and deep hollows of his cheeks, the dark stubble on his chin, and the fine lines that fanned out from his eyes. The dim light couldn't hide his rough-edged good looks.

He'd be an interesting subject to paint. Or better yet, to capture in charcoal.

He raised an eyebrow and she dropped her gaze, heat creeping up her neck and into her cheeks. She could sense his restless energy, the restless energy of her sisters, who hovered at edge of the woods. By the time she finally managed to remove her skates and pull on her mukluks, her heart was pounding with anxiety, her stomach twisting with nerves. *Murder.* Just the word filled her with dread.

"Are we ready?" Rissa grabbed the skates up from where Portia had dropped them. "I'm freezing."

"Me, too." Portia stood, started to follow her retreating sister and was pulled up short by a tug on her skirt. A jagged piece of wood had caught the silky material and she leaned down to free it as icy wind blasted across the clearing, knifing through the clothes she'd layered herself in. She shivered as she tugged at the cloth.

"Let me help." The masculine voice sounded so close to her ear Portia jumped, turning to face the detective who stood just inches away. His eyes were even bluer than she'd thought, his hair a short, spiky golden-brown that looked like it would be soft to the touch.

That she would even think such a thing had

Portia stepping back, dropping her eyes away from his. “I thought you’d gone on ahead.”

“And left you out here by yourself?”

“It wouldn’t be the first time I’d been out here alone.”

“But it may be the first time you’ve been out here alone while a murderer wanders free.”

Love Inspired®
SUSPENSE
RIVETING INSPIRATIONAL ROMANCE

RITA® Award-winning author

GAYLE ROPER

makes her Love Inspired Suspense debut with

SEE NO EVIL

Young artist Anna Volente has a near-death experience, but with the help of her handsome protector, Gray Edwards, she learns that life's greatest fulfillment is achieved by using the talents God has given her and following her heart both professionally and personally.

Available February 2007 wherever you buy books.

Steeple Hill®

www.SteepleHill.com

LISSNE

Love Inspired®
SUSPENSE
RIVETING INSPIRATIONAL ROMANCE

Don't miss the intrigue and the romance in this six-book family saga.

Six sisters face murder, mayhem and mystery while unraveling the past.

FATAL IMAGE
Lenora Worth
January 2007

LITTLE GIRL LOST
Shirlee McCoy
February 2007

BELOVED ENEMY
Terri Reed
March 2007

THE SOUND OF SECRETS
Irene Brand
April 2007

DEADLY PAYOFF
Valerie Hansen
May 2007

WHERE THE TRUTH LIES
Lynn Bulock
June 2007

Available wherever you buy books.

www.SteepleHill.com

LISSOSLIST

Love Inspired®
SUSPENSE
RIVETING INSPIRATIONAL ROMANCE

Six sisters face murder, mayhem and mystery while unraveling the past.

Little Girl Lost

SHIRLEE McCOY

Book 2 of the multiauthor The Secrets of Stoneley miniseries.

Portia Blanchard had been planning to spend time with police detective Mick Campbell to keep tabs on the family investigation, but she soon finds herself drawn to him. Is it because he's a single dad or because his faith is strong under fire?

Available February 2007 wherever you buy books.

www.SteepleHill.com

LISLGL

REQUEST YOUR FREE BOOKS!

2 FREE INSPIRATIONAL NOVELS PLUS 2 FREE MYSTERY GIFTS

Love Inspired®

YES! Please send me 2 FREE Love Inspired® novels and my 2 FREE mystery gifts. After receiving them, if I don't wish to receive any more books, I can return the shipping statement marked "cancel." If I don't cancel, I will receive 4 brand-new novels every month and be billed just $3.99 per book in the U.S., or $4.74 per book in Canada, plus 25¢ shipping and handling per book and applicable taxes, if any*. That's a savings of 20% off the cover price! I understand that accepting the 2 free books and gifts places me under no obligation to buy anything. I can always return a shipment and cancel at any time. Even if I never buy another book from Steeple Hill, the two free books and gifts are mine to keep forever.

113 IDN EF26 313 IDN EF27

Name (PLEASE PRINT)

Address Apt. #

City State/Prov. Zip/Postal Code

Signature (if under 18, a parent or guardian must sign)

Order online at www.LoveInspiredBooks.com

Or mail to Steeple Hill Reader Service™:

IN U.S.A.: P.O. Box 1867, Buffalo, NY 14240-1867

IN CANADA: P.O. Box 609, Fort Erie, Ontario L2A 5X3

Not valid to current Love Inspired subscribers.

Want to try two free books from another series?
Call 1-800-873-8635 or visit www.morefreebooks.com

* Terms and prices subject to change without notice. NY residents add applicable sales tax. Canadian residents will be charged applicable provincial taxes and GST. This offer is limited to one order per household. All orders subject to approval. Credit or debit balances in a customer's account(s) may be offset by any other outstanding balance owed by or to the customer. Please allow 4 to 6 weeks for delivery.

Your Privacy: Steeple Hill is committed to protecting your privacy. Our Privacy Policy is available online at www.eHarlequin.com or upon request from the Reader Service. From time to time we make our lists of customers available to reputable firms who may have a product or service of interest to you. If you would prefer we not share your name and address, please check here. ☐

LIREG07